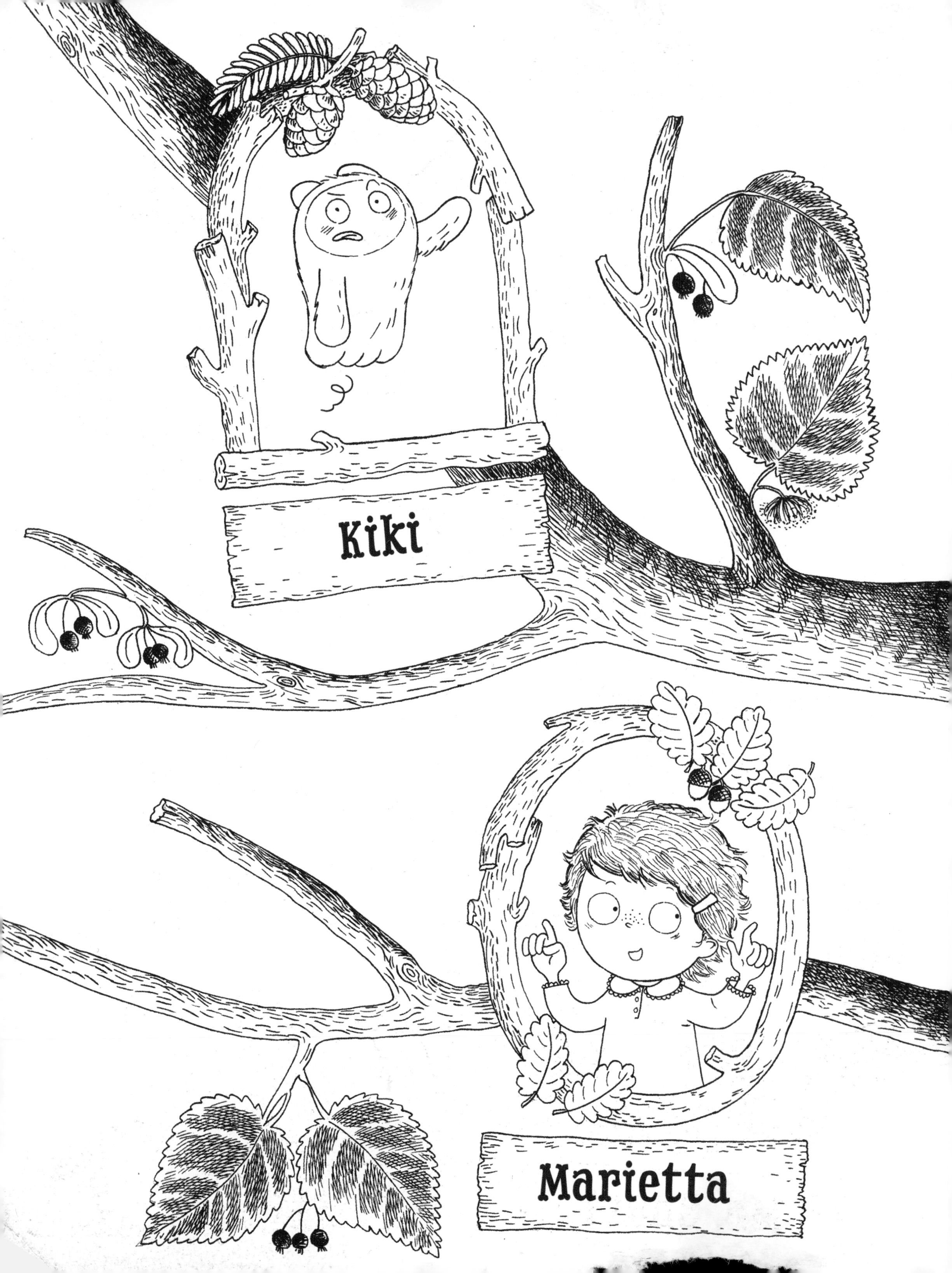
Kiki
Marietta

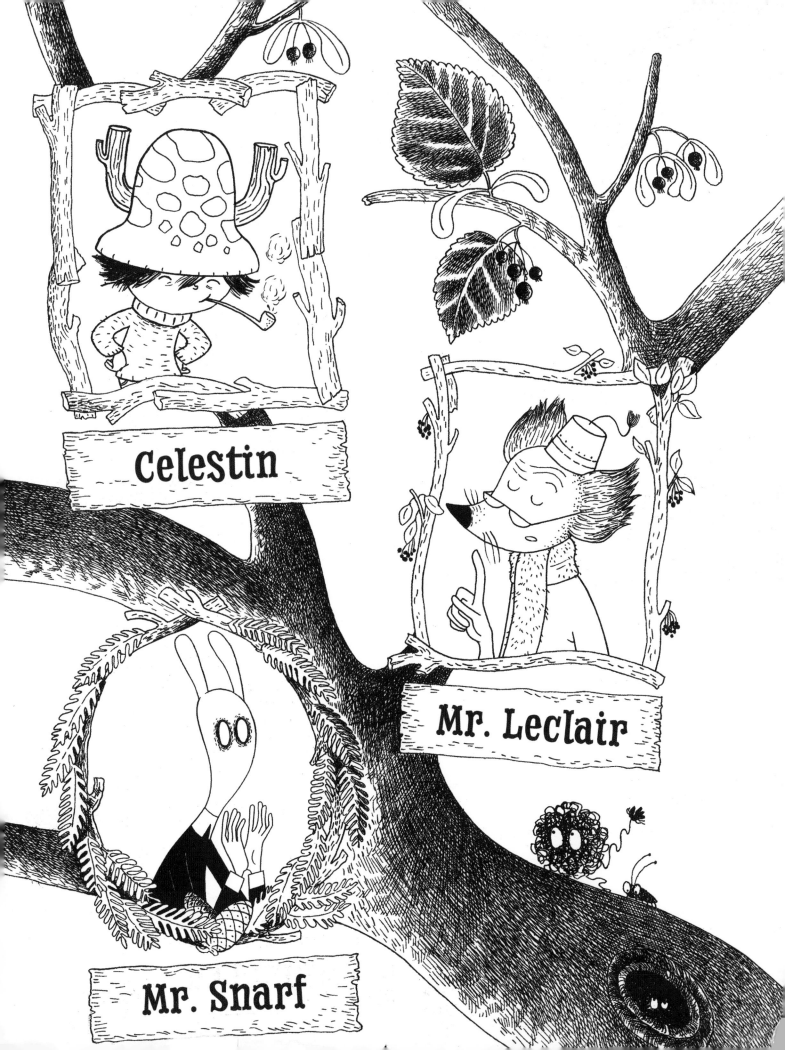

Celestin

Mr. Leclair

Mr. Snarf

HOTEL STRANGE

On the Sapphire's Trail #2

Florian and Katherine Ferrier

illustrations and coloring by Katherine Ferrier

Graphic Universe™ • Minneapolis

Story by Florian and Katherine Ferrier
Illustrations and coloring by Katherine Ferrier
Translation by Carol Klio Burrell

This work received the support of La Cité internationale de la bande dessinée et de l'image (comics museum, library, and arts complex) through an author residency at La maison des auteurs in Angoulême, France.

First American edition published in 2016 by Graphic Universe™

Copyright © 2011 by Sarbacane, Paris
Published by arrangement with Sylvain Coissard Agency in cooperation with Nicolas Grivel Agency

Graphic Universe™ is a trademark of Lerner Publishing Group, Inc.

Graphic Universe™
A division of Lerner Publishing Group, Inc.
241 First Avenue North
Minneapolis, MN 55401 USA

For reading levels and more information, look up this title at www.lernerbooks.com.

Main body text set in Andy Std Bold 12.5/13.5. Typeface provided by Monotype.

Library of Congress Cataloging-in-Publication Data

Ferrier, Katherine, author, illustrator.
    On the sapphire's trail / author: Katherine Ferrier, Florian Ferrier ; illustrator: Katherine Ferrier.
        pages cm — (Hotel Strange ; #02)
    Summary: "The characters of Hotel Strange are busy planning a music festival, until thieves kidnap Marietta and Mr. Leclair. Kiki and the others must solve the mystery of a missing sapphire to save their friends, and the festival!" —Provided by publisher.
    ISBN 978-1-4677-8585-3 (lb : alk. paper) — ISBN 978-1-4677-9573-9 (pb : alk. paper) — ISBN 978-1-4677-9574-6 (eb pdf)
    1. Graphic novels. [1. Graphic novels. 2. Kidnapping—Fiction. 3. Festivals—Fiction. 4. Mystery and detective stories.] I. Ferrier, Florian, author II. Ferrier, Katherine, illustrator III. Title.
PZ7.7.F48On 2015
741.5'973—dc23   2015016193

Manufactured in the United States of America
1 – VP – 12/31/15

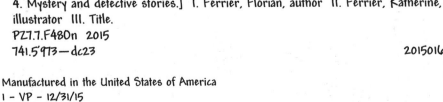

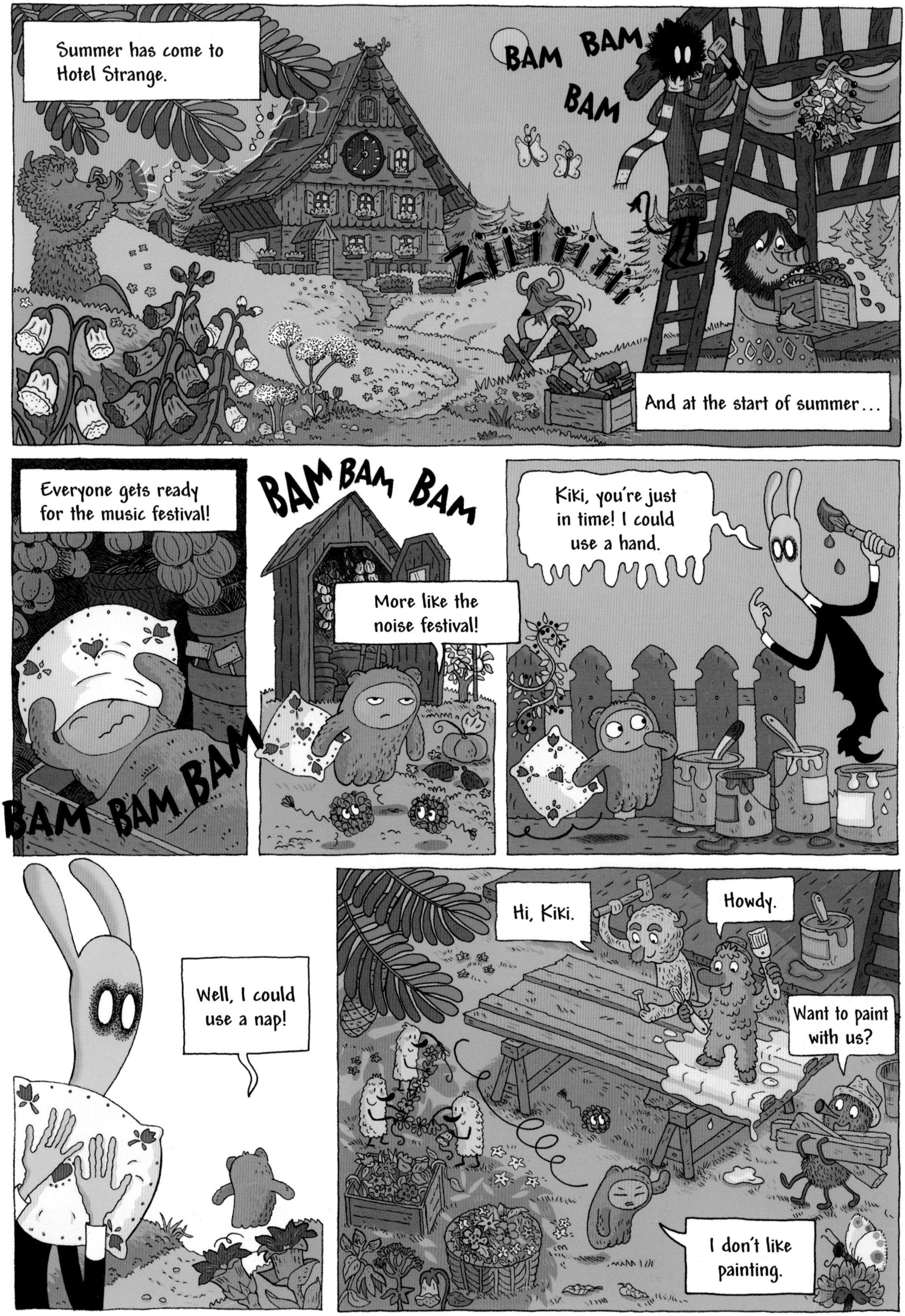

Summer has come to Hotel Strange.
BAM BAM
BAM
ZIIIIIIII
And at the start of summer...
Everyone gets ready for the music festival!
BAM BAM BAM
BAM BAM BAM
More like the noise festival!
Kiki, you're just in time! I could use a hand.
Well, I could use a nap!
Hi, Kiki.
Howdy.
Want to paint with us?
I don't like painting.

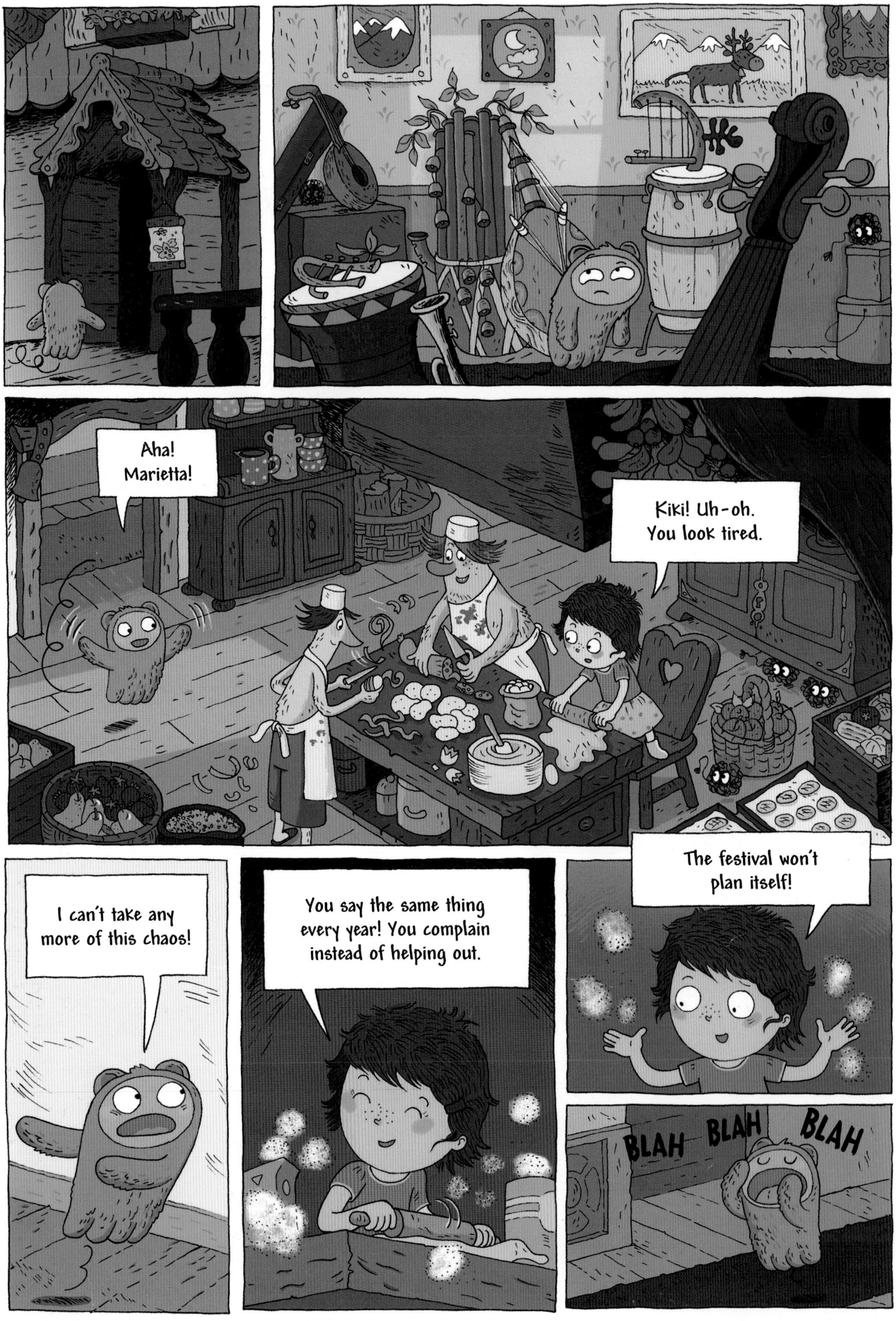
Aha! Marietta!
Kiki! Uh-oh. You look tired.
I can't take any more of this chaos!
You say the same thing every year! You complain instead of helping out.
The festival won't plan itself!
BLAH BLAH BLAH

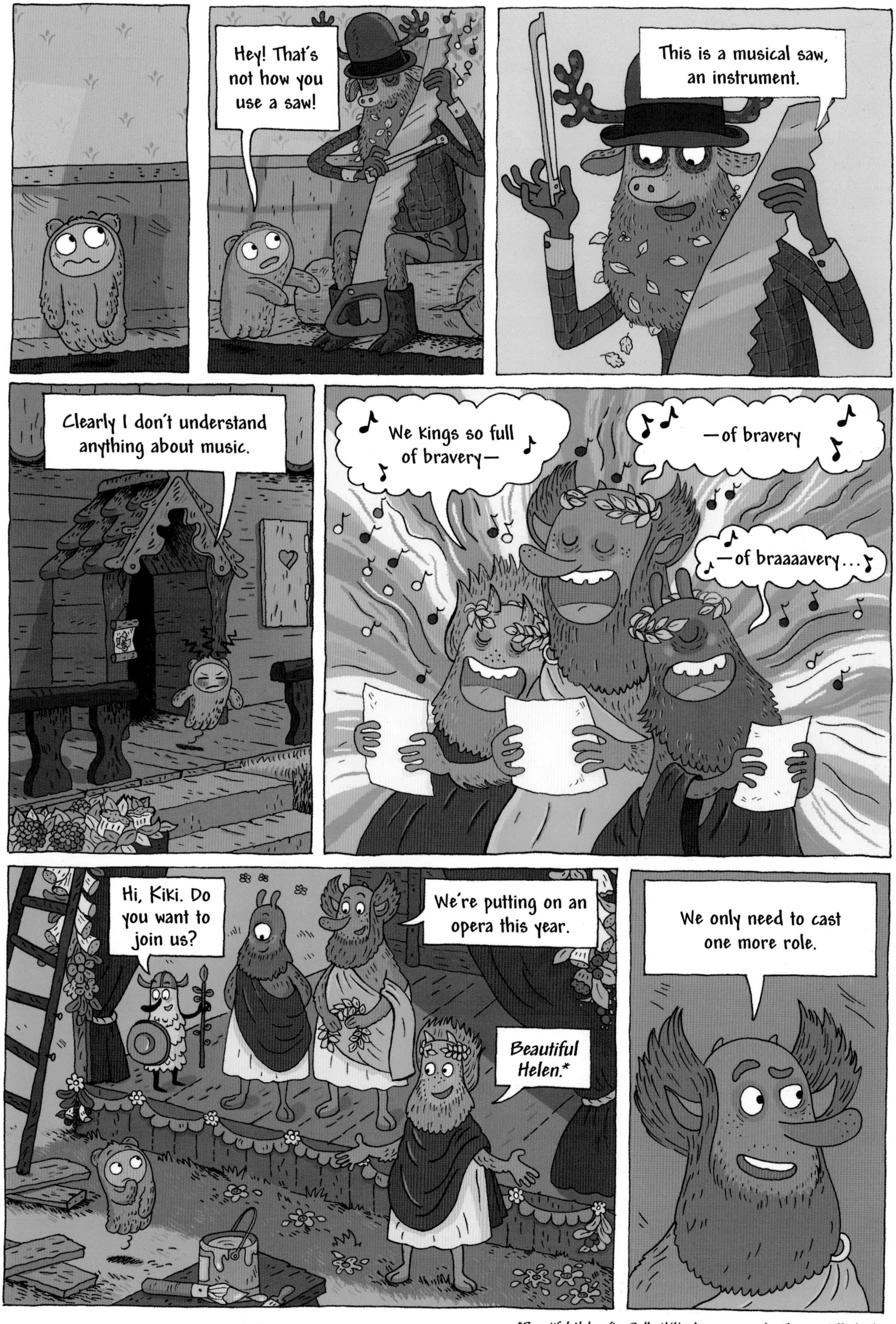
Hey! That's not how you use a saw!
This is a musical saw, an instrument.
Clearly I don't understand anything about music.
We kings so full of bravery—
—of bravery
—of braaaavery...
Hi, Kiki. Do you want to join us?
We're putting on an opera this year.
*Beautiful Helen.**
We only need to cast one more role.

Beautiful Helen (La Belle Hélène) is an opera by Jacques Offenbach.

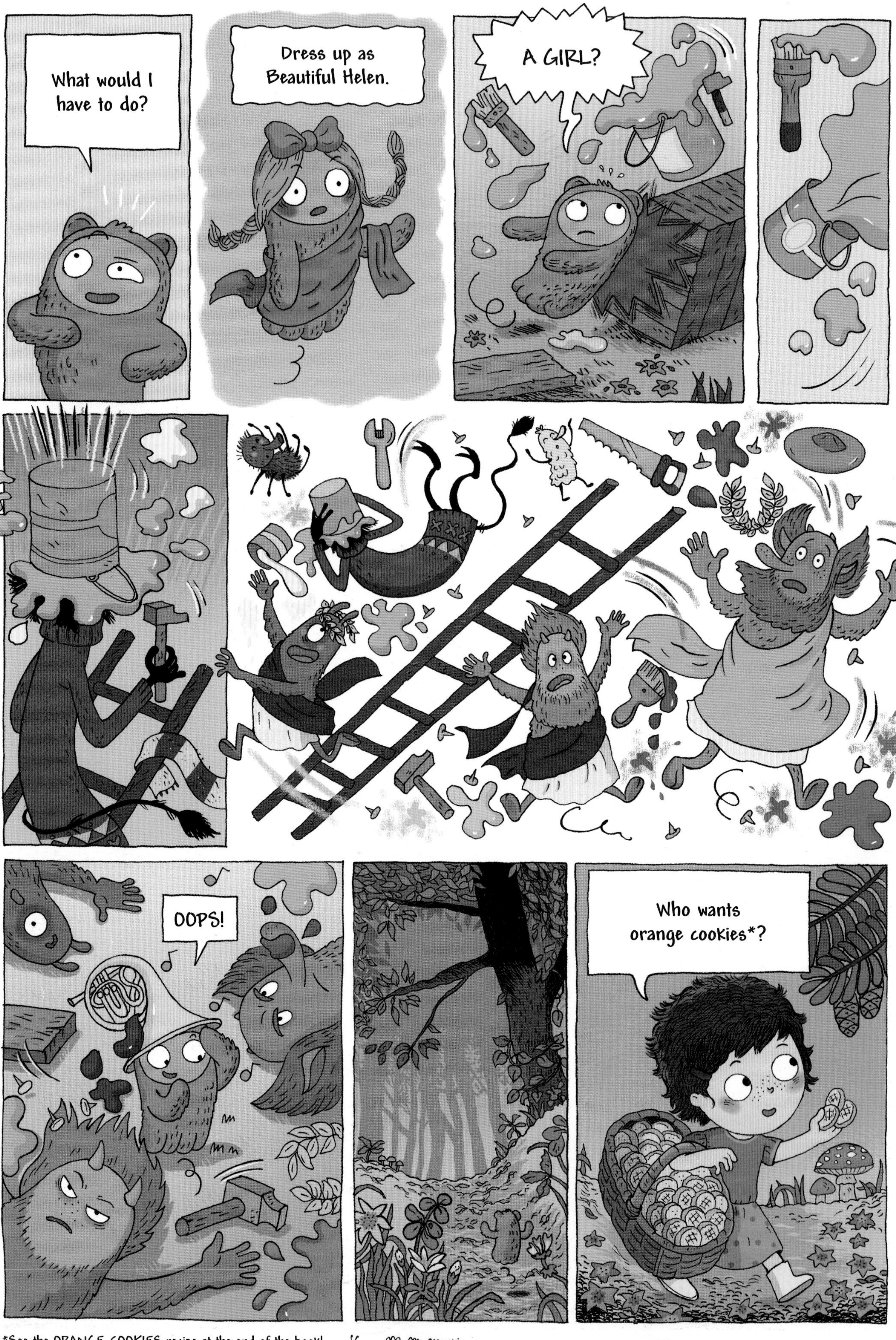
What would I have to do?
Dress up as Beautiful Helen.
A GIRL?
OOPS!
Who wants orange cookies*?

*See the ORANGE COOKIES recipe at the end of the book!

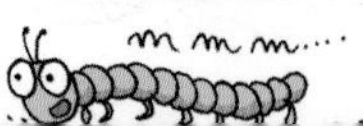
m m m....

I do!

I do!

I do!

Here you go, Mr. Leclair!

I can't say no to a treat.

Kiki...

We need...

some yellow paint...

some wood glue...

and some needles and thread to make a garland.

A A A A A A H H

He really doesn't like to work.

You could help us, lazy bum!

Every time I try to help...

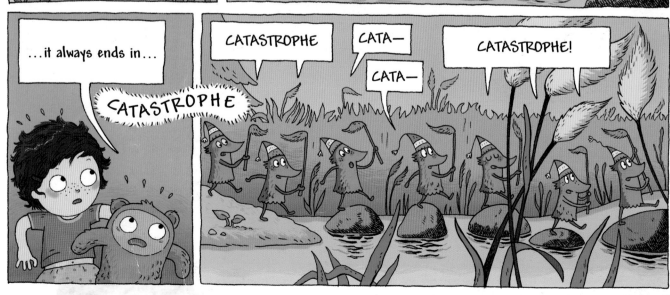

...it always ends in...

CATASTROPHE

CATASTROPHE

CATA—

CATA—

CATASTROPHE!

7

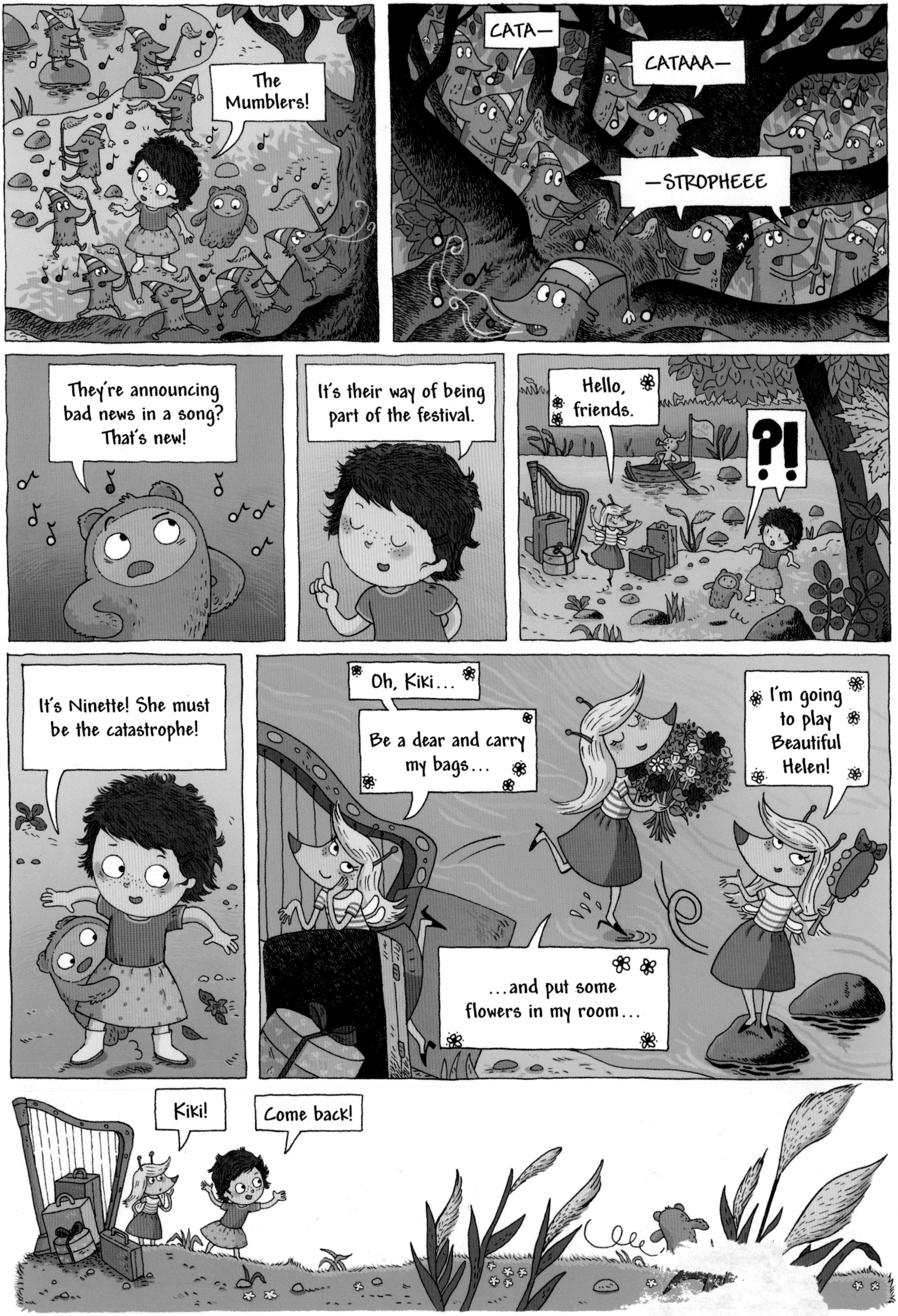

The Mumblers!
CATA—
CATAAA—
—STROPHEEE
They're announcing bad news in a song? That's new!
It's their way of being part of the festival.
Hello, friends.
?!
It's Ninette! She must be the catastrophe!
Oh, Kiki...
Be a dear and carry my bags...
...and put some flowers in my room...
I'm going to play Beautiful Helen!
Kiki!
Come back!

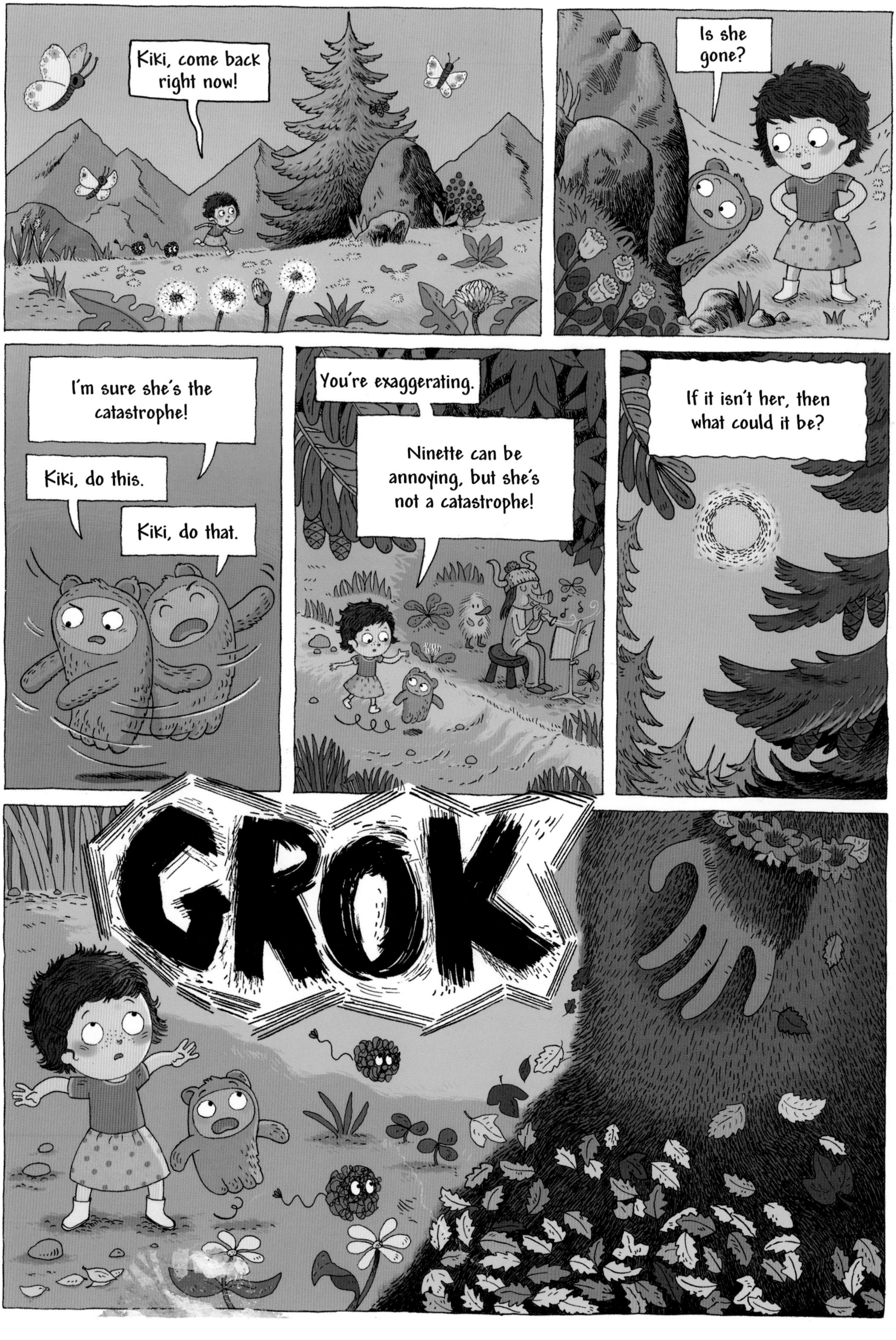
Kiki, come back right now!
Is she gone?
I'm sure she's the catastrophe!
Kiki, do this.
Kiki, do that.
You're exaggerating.
Ninette can be annoying, but she's not a catastrophe!
If it isn't her, then what could it be?
GROK

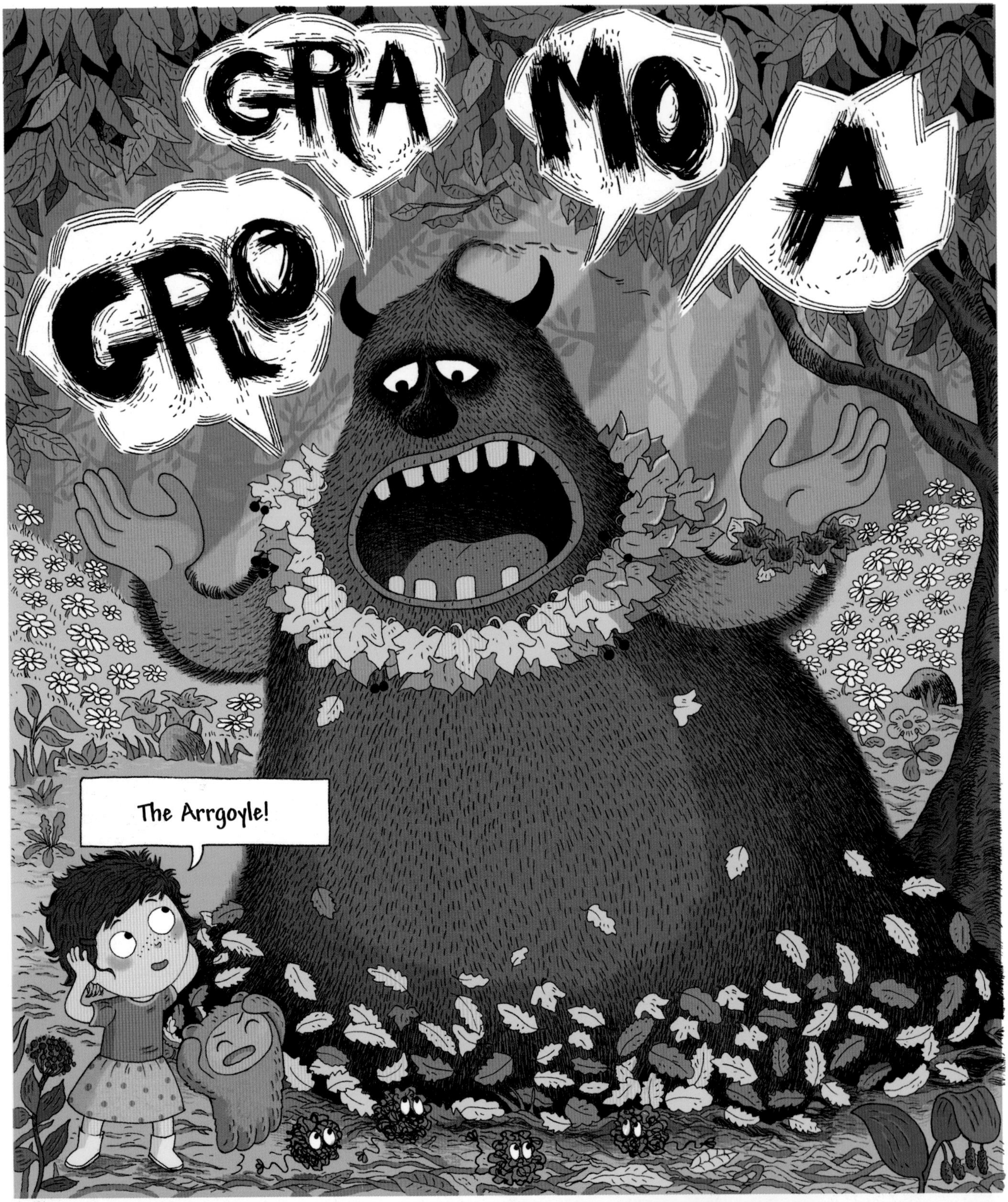
GRO
GRA
MO
A
The Arrgoyle!

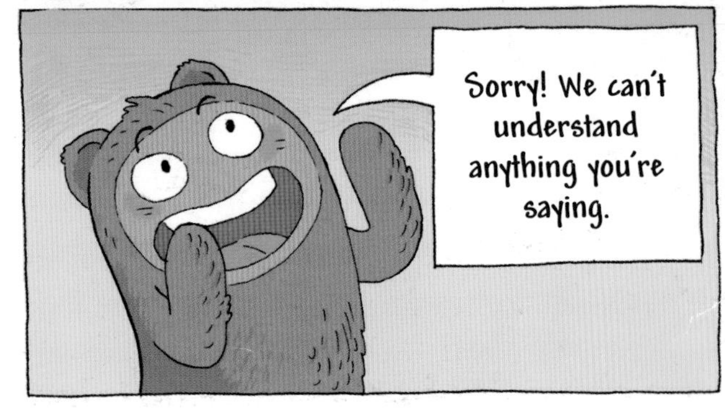
Sorry! We can't understand anything you're saying.

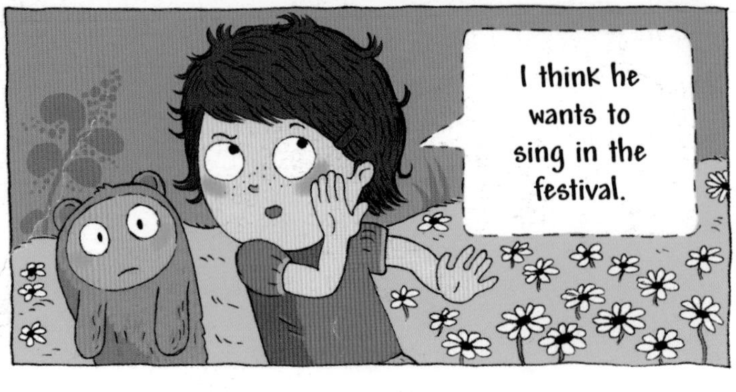
I think he wants to sing in the festival.

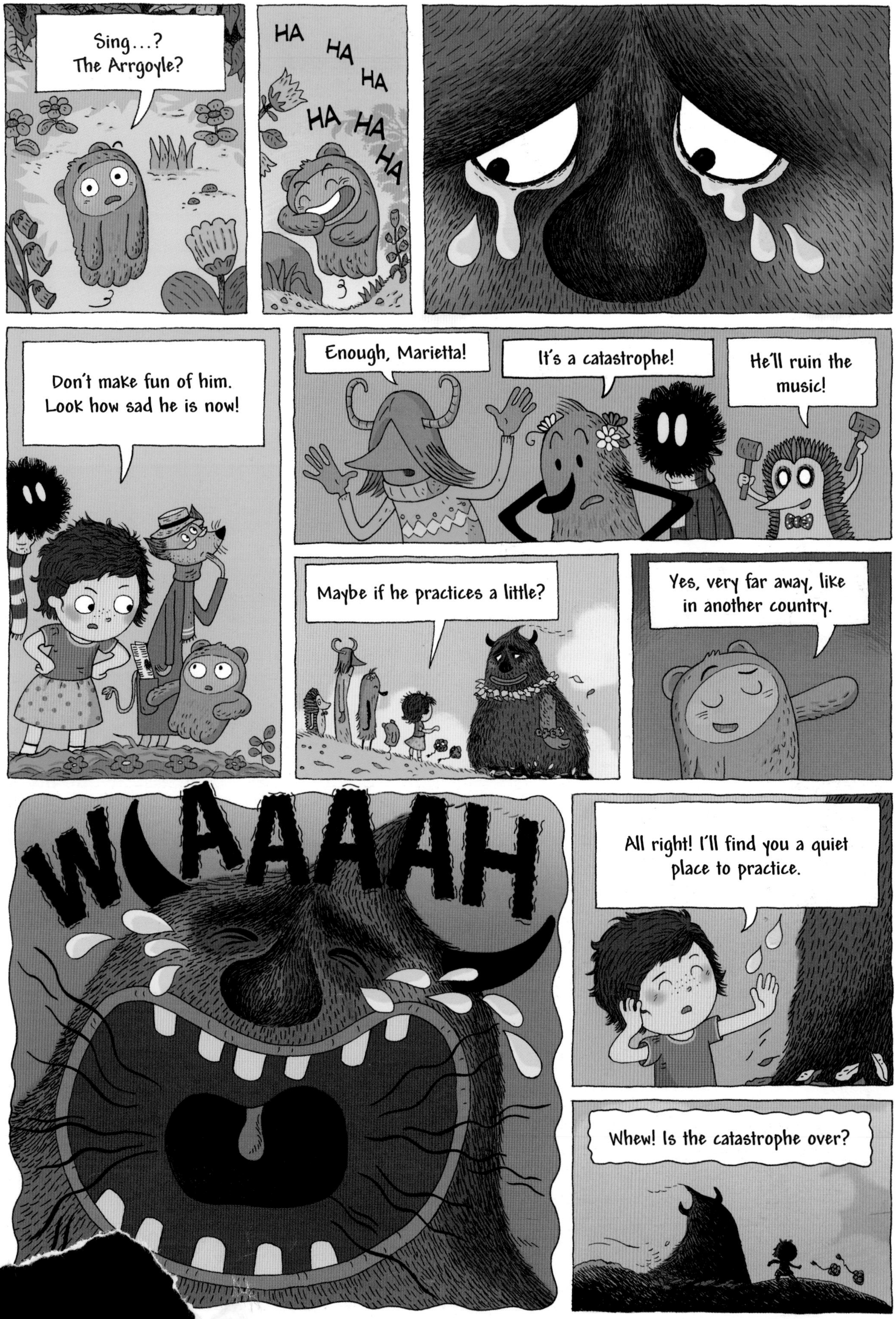
Sing...?
The Arrgoyle?
HA HA HA HA HA HA
Don't make fun of him. Look how sad he is now!
Enough, Marietta!
It's a catastrophe!
He'll ruin the music!
Maybe if he practices a little?
Yes, very far away, like in another country.
WAAAAH
All right! I'll find you a quiet place to practice.
Whew! Is the catastrophe over?

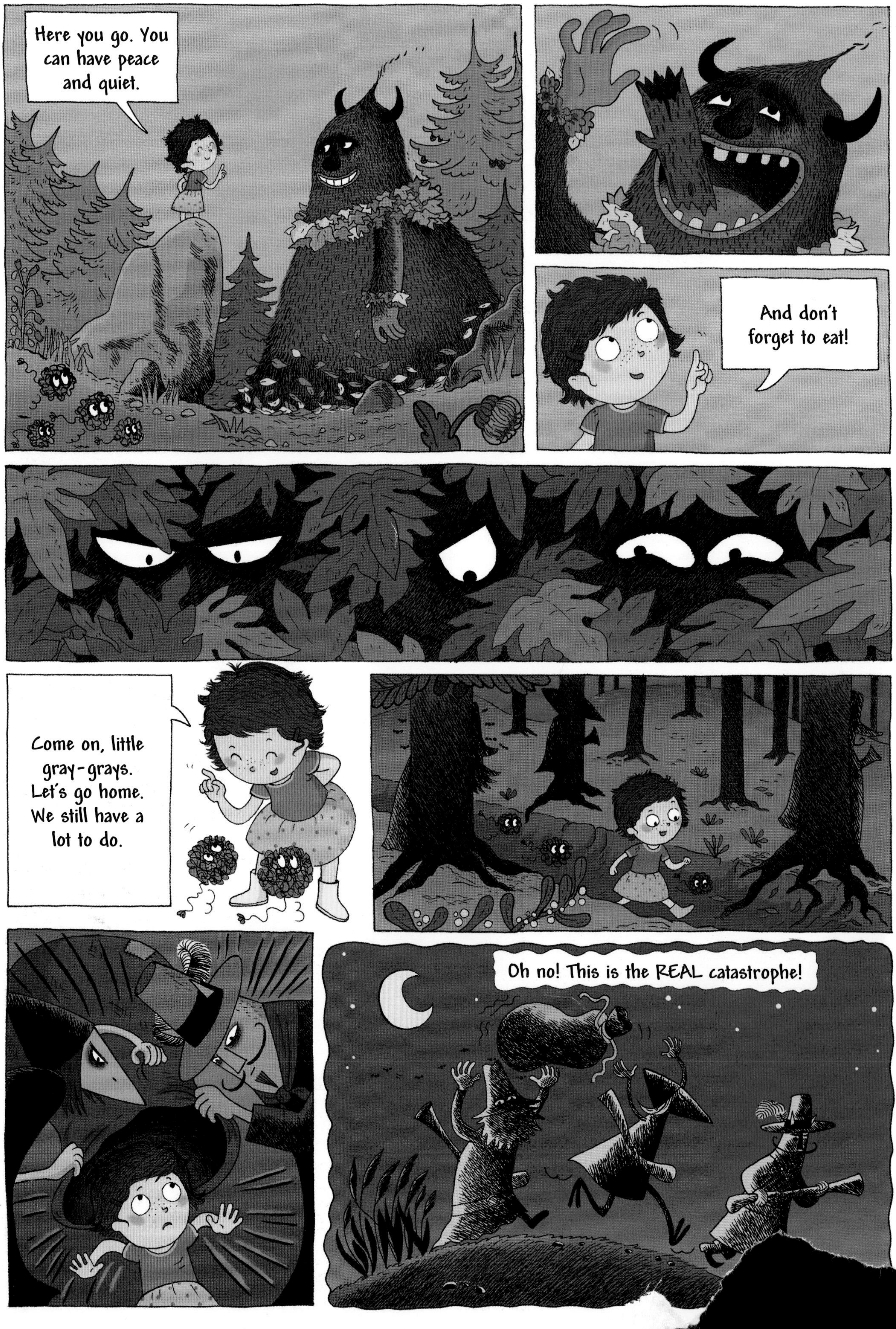
Here you go. You can have peace and quiet.
And don't forget to eat!
Come on, little gray-grays. Let's go home. We still have a lot to do.
Oh no! This is the REAL catastrophe!

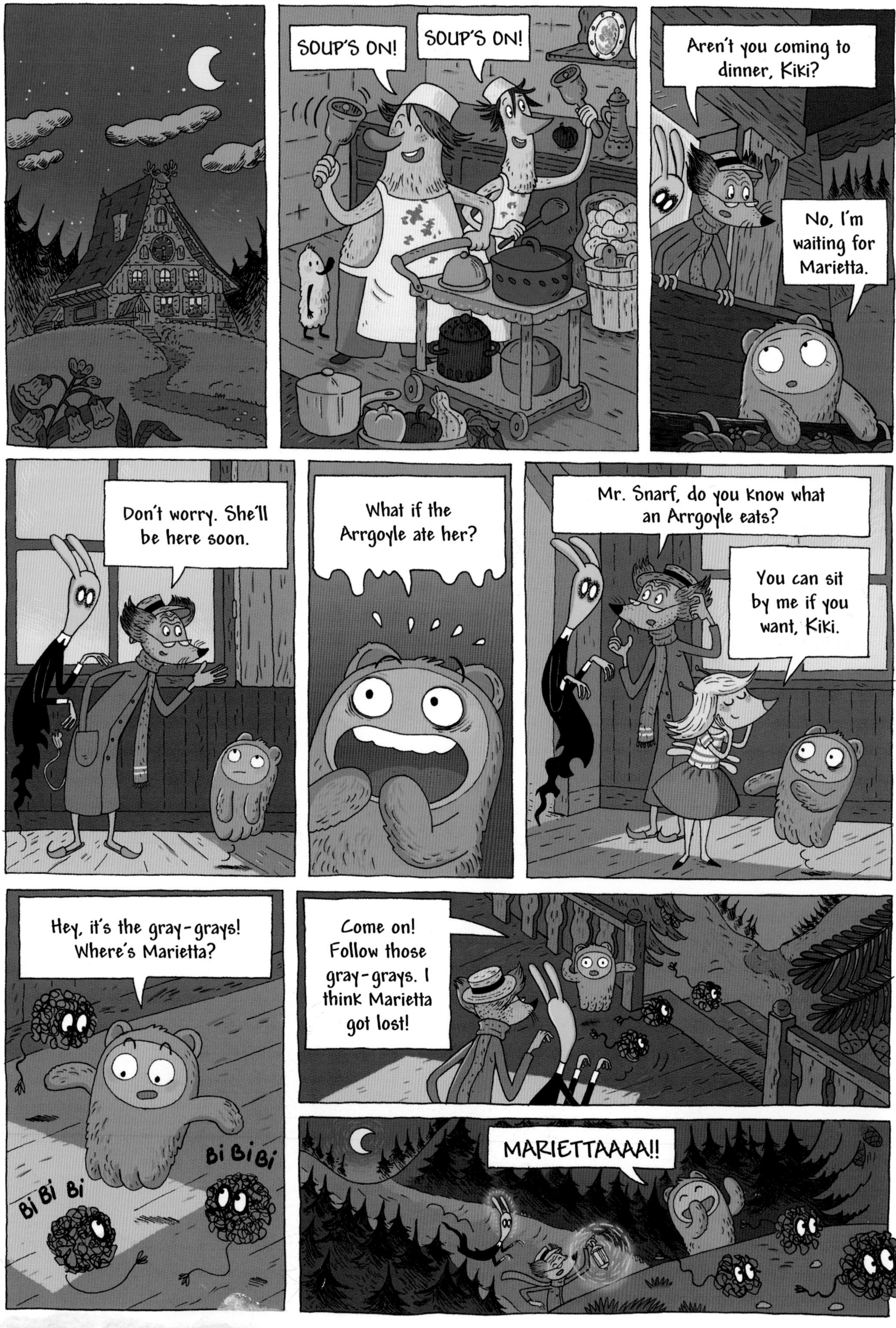
SOUP'S ON!
SOUP'S ON!
Aren't you coming to dinner, Kiki?
No, I'm waiting for Marietta.
Don't worry. She'll be here soon.
What if the Arrgoyle ate her?
Mr. Snarf, do you know what an Arrgoyle eats?
You can sit by me if you want, Kiki.
Hey, it's the gray-grays! Where's Marietta?
Bi Bi Bi
Bi Bi Bi
Come on! Follow those gray-grays. I think Marietta got lost!
MARIETTAAAA!!

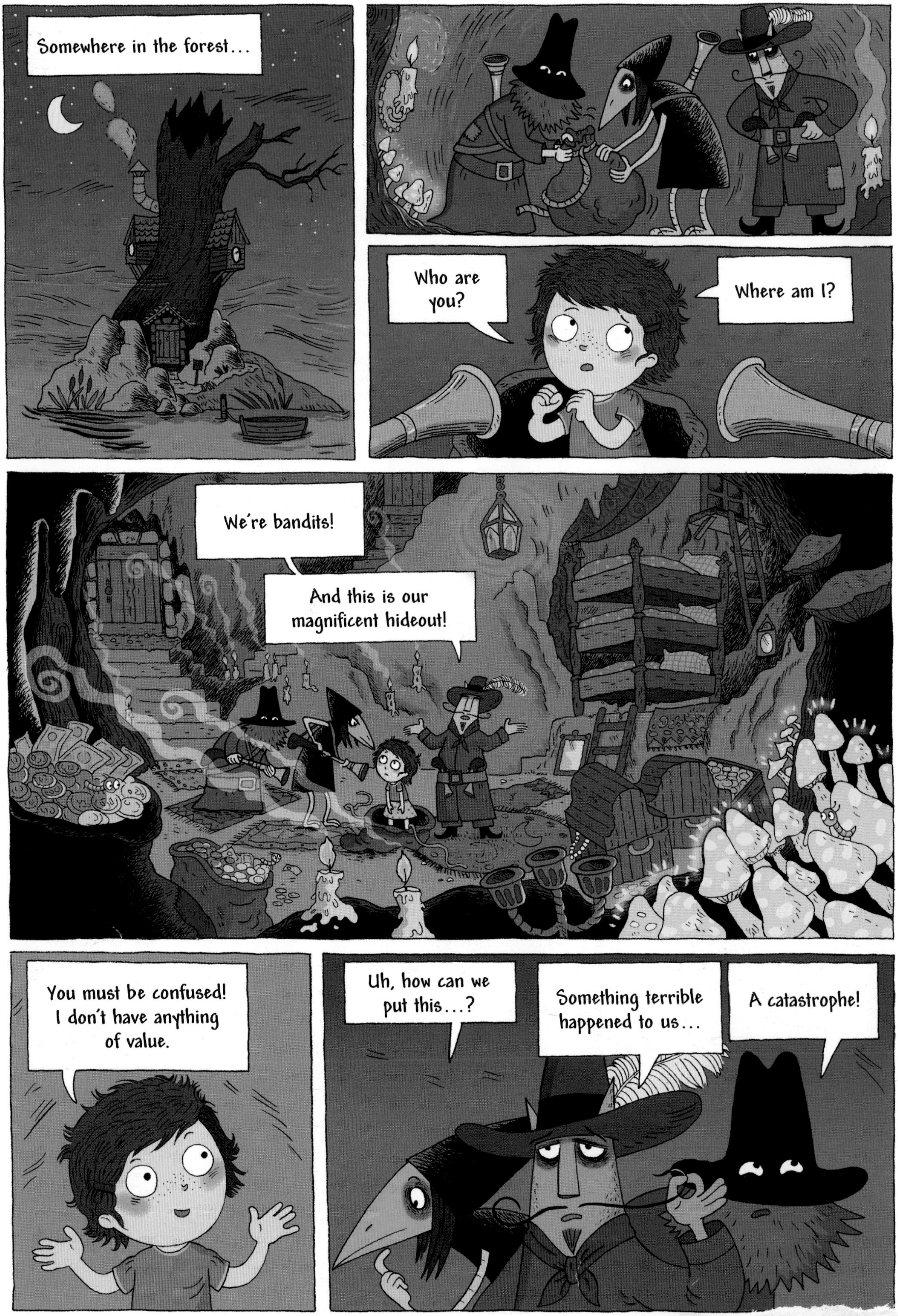
Somewhere in the forest...
Who are you?
Where am I?
We're bandits!
And this is our magnificent hideout!
You must be confused! I don't have anything of value.
Uh, how can we put this...?
Something terrible happened to us...
A catastrophe!

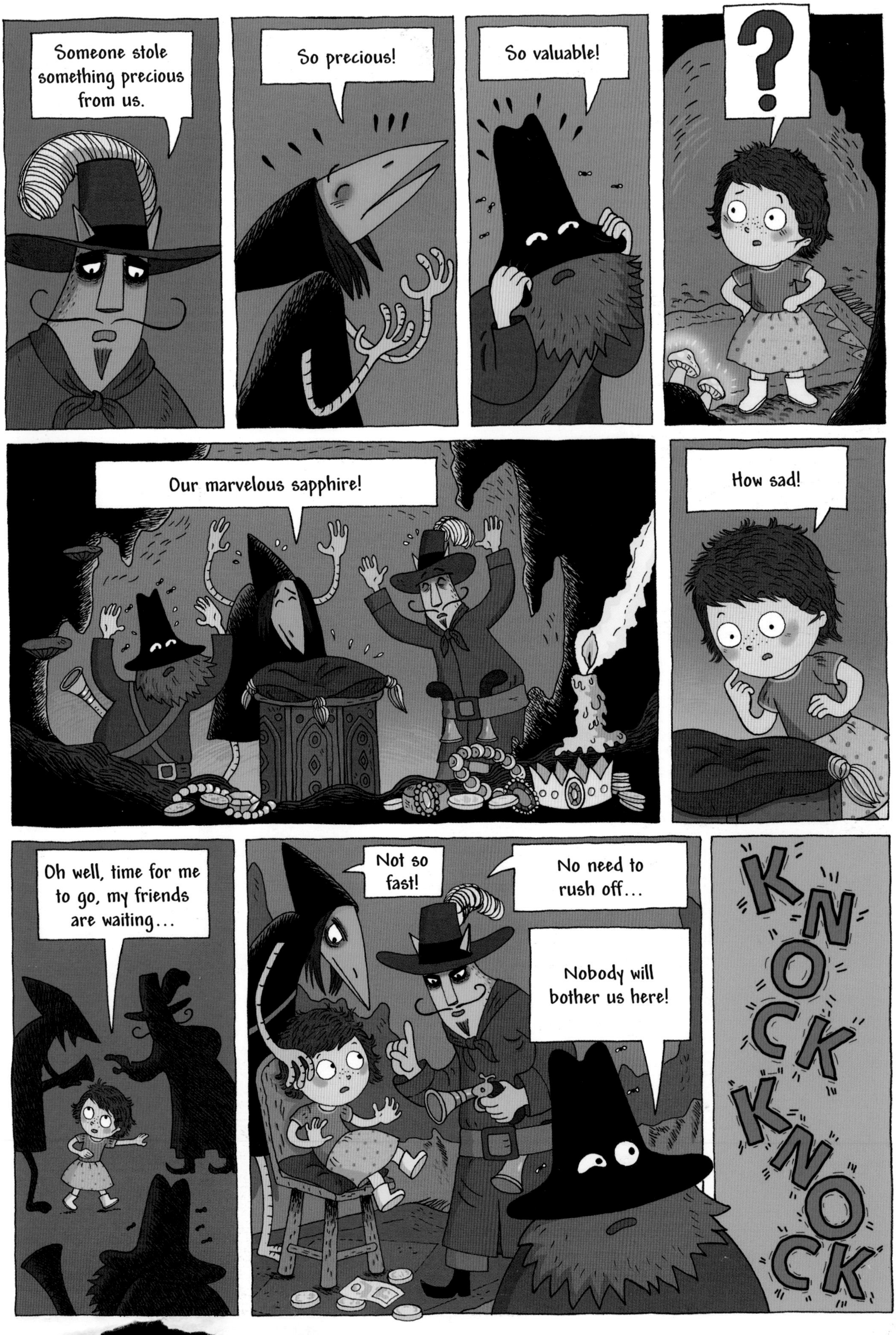
Someone stole something precious from us.
So precious!
So valuable!
?
Our marvelous sapphire!
How sad!
Oh well, time for me to go, my friends are waiting...
Not so fast!
No need to rush off...
Nobody will bother us here!
KNOCK KNOCK

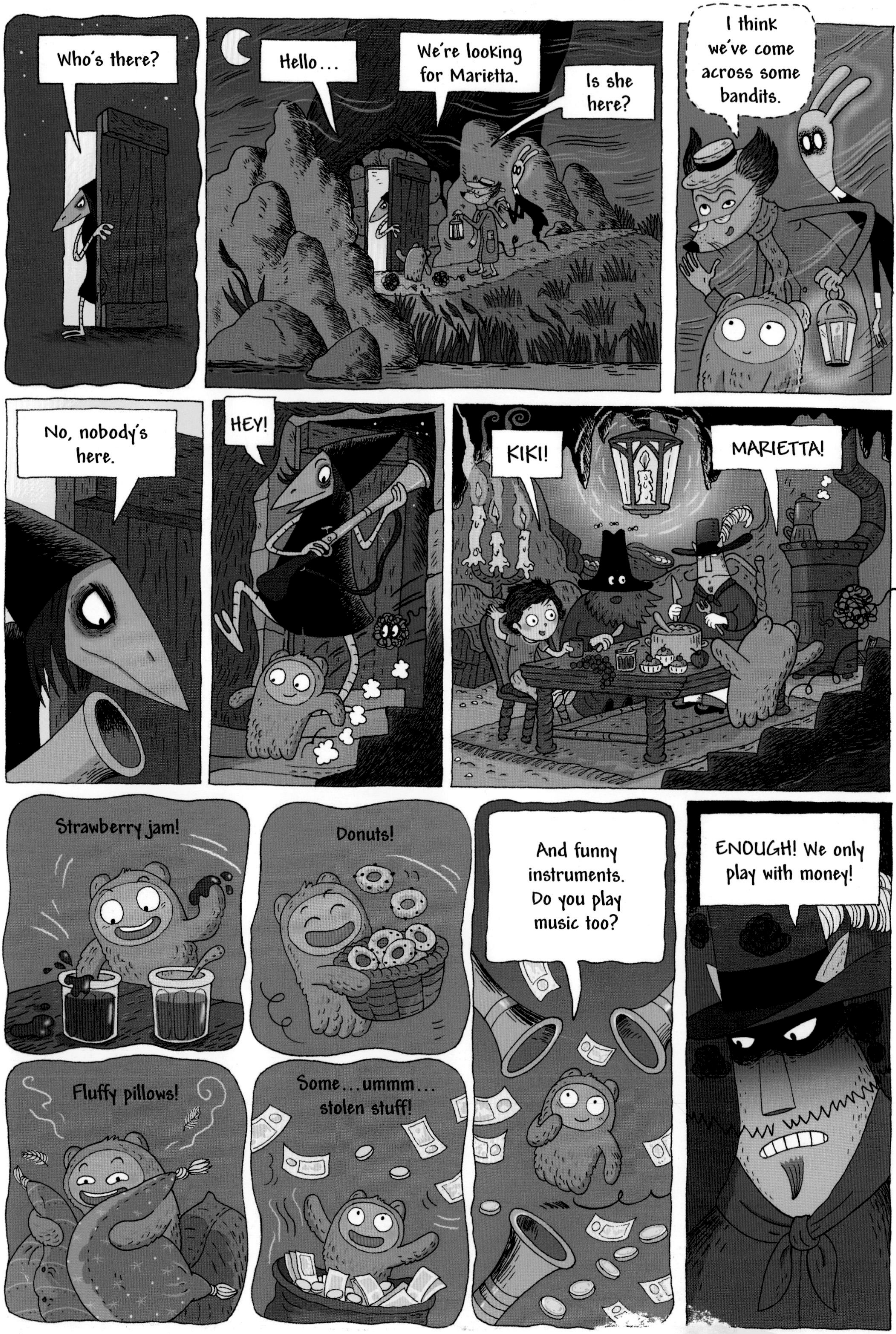

Who's there?
Hello...
We're looking for Marietta.
Is she here?
I think we've come across some bandits.
No, nobody's here.
HEY!
KIKI!
MARIETTA!
Strawberry jam!
Donuts!
Fluffy pillows!
Some... ummm... stolen stuff!
And funny instruments. Do you play music too?
ENOUGH! We only play with money!

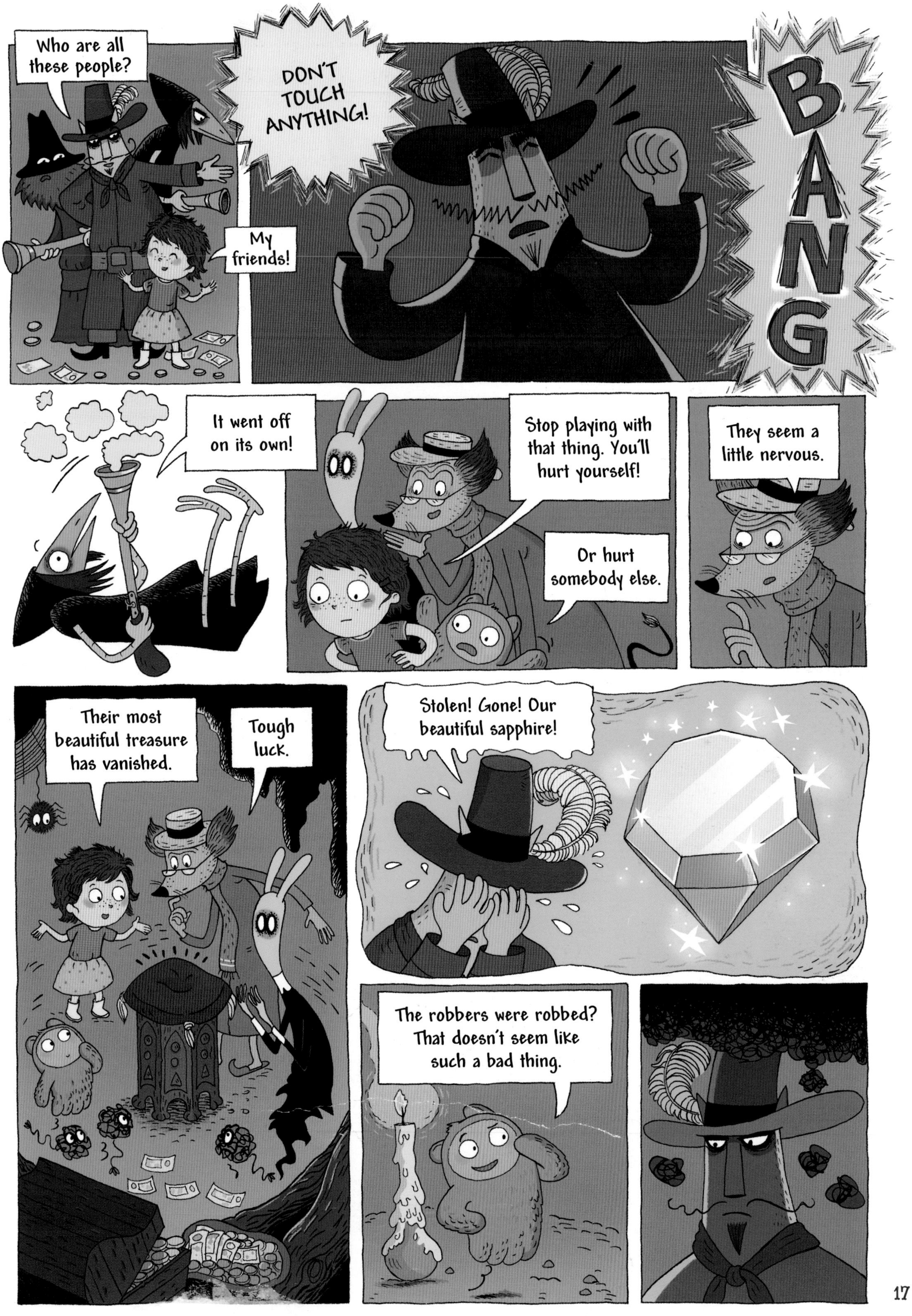

Who are all these people?
DON'T TOUCH ANYTHING!
My friends!
BANG
It went off on its own!
Stop playing with that thing. You'll hurt yourself!
Or hurt somebody else.
They seem a little nervous.
Their most beautiful treasure has vanished.
Tough luck.
Stolen! Gone! Our beautiful sapphire!
The robbers were robbed? That doesn't seem like such a bad thing.

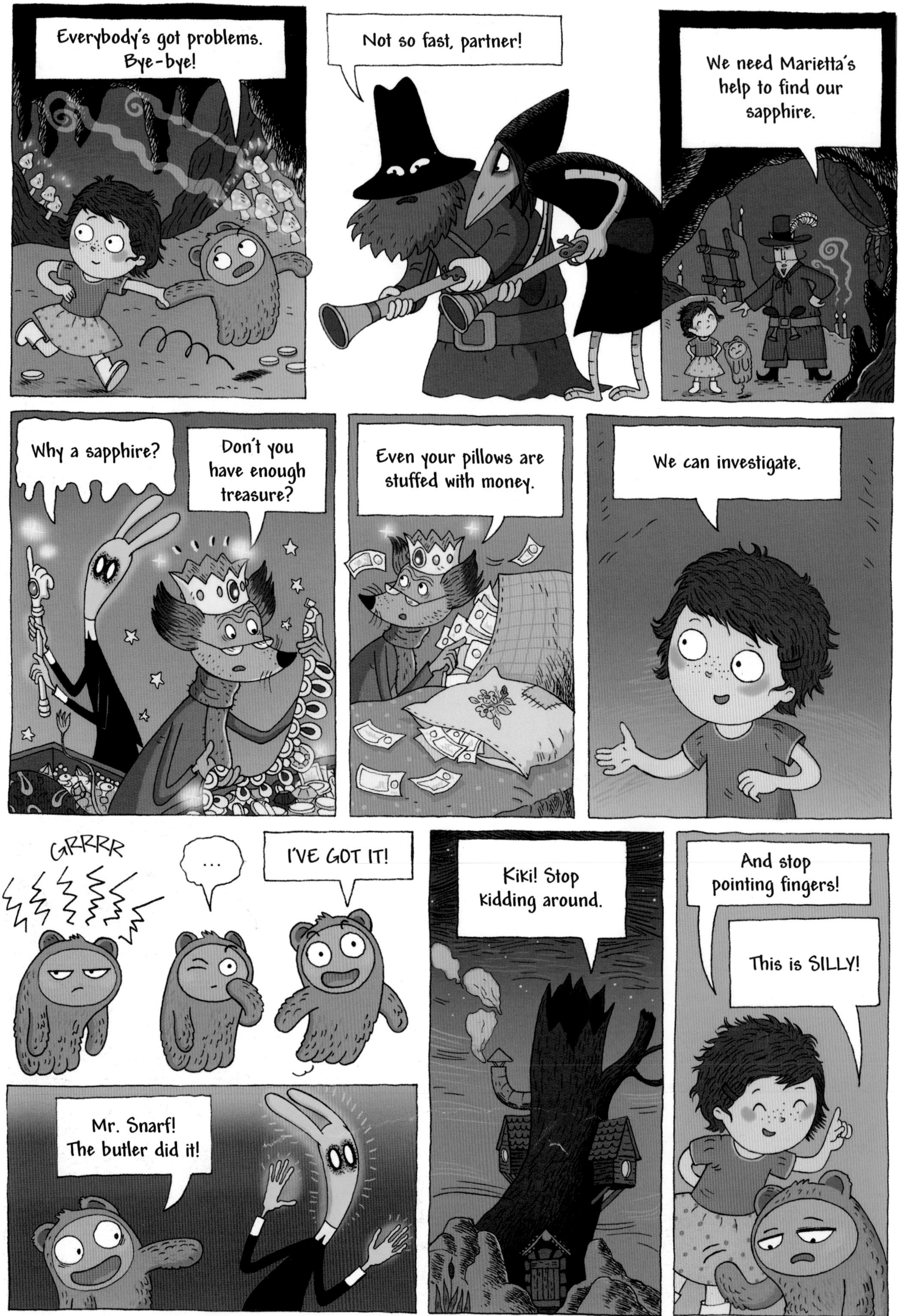

Everybody's got problems. Bye-bye!
Not so fast, partner!
We need Marietta's help to find our sapphire.
Why a sapphire?
Don't you have enough treasure?
Even your pillows are stuffed with money.
We can investigate.
GRRRR
...
I'VE GOT IT!
Mr. Snarf! The butler did it!
Kiki! Stop kidding around.
And stop pointing fingers!
This is SILLY!

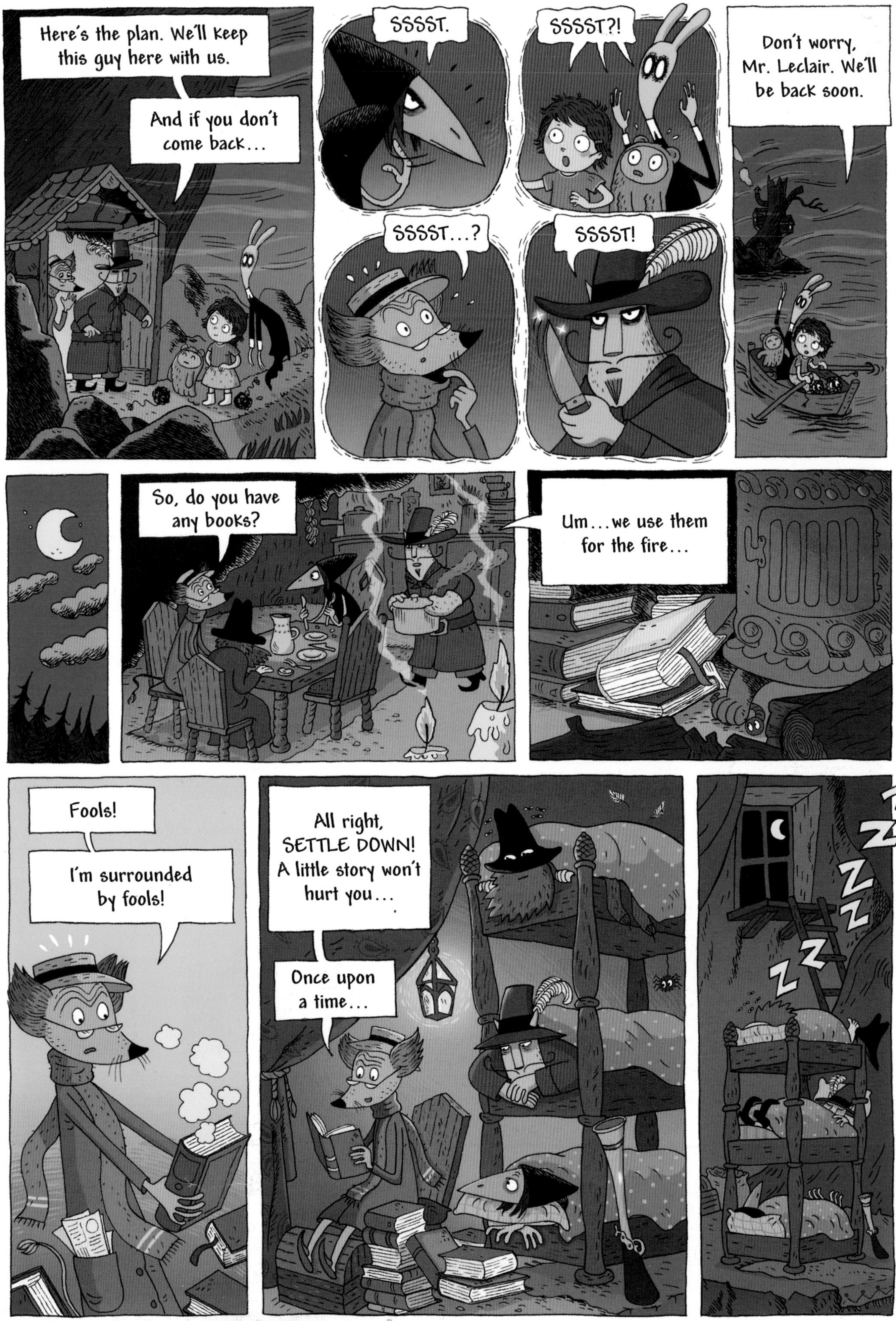

Here's the plan. We'll keep this guy here with us.
And if you don't come back...
SSSST.
SSSST?!
Don't worry, Mr. Leclair. We'll be back soon.
SSSST...?
SSSST!
So, do you have any books?
Um...we use them for the fire...
Fools!
I'm surrounded by fools!
All right, SETTLE DOWN! A little story won't hurt you...
Once upon a time...
Z Z Z Z Z Z

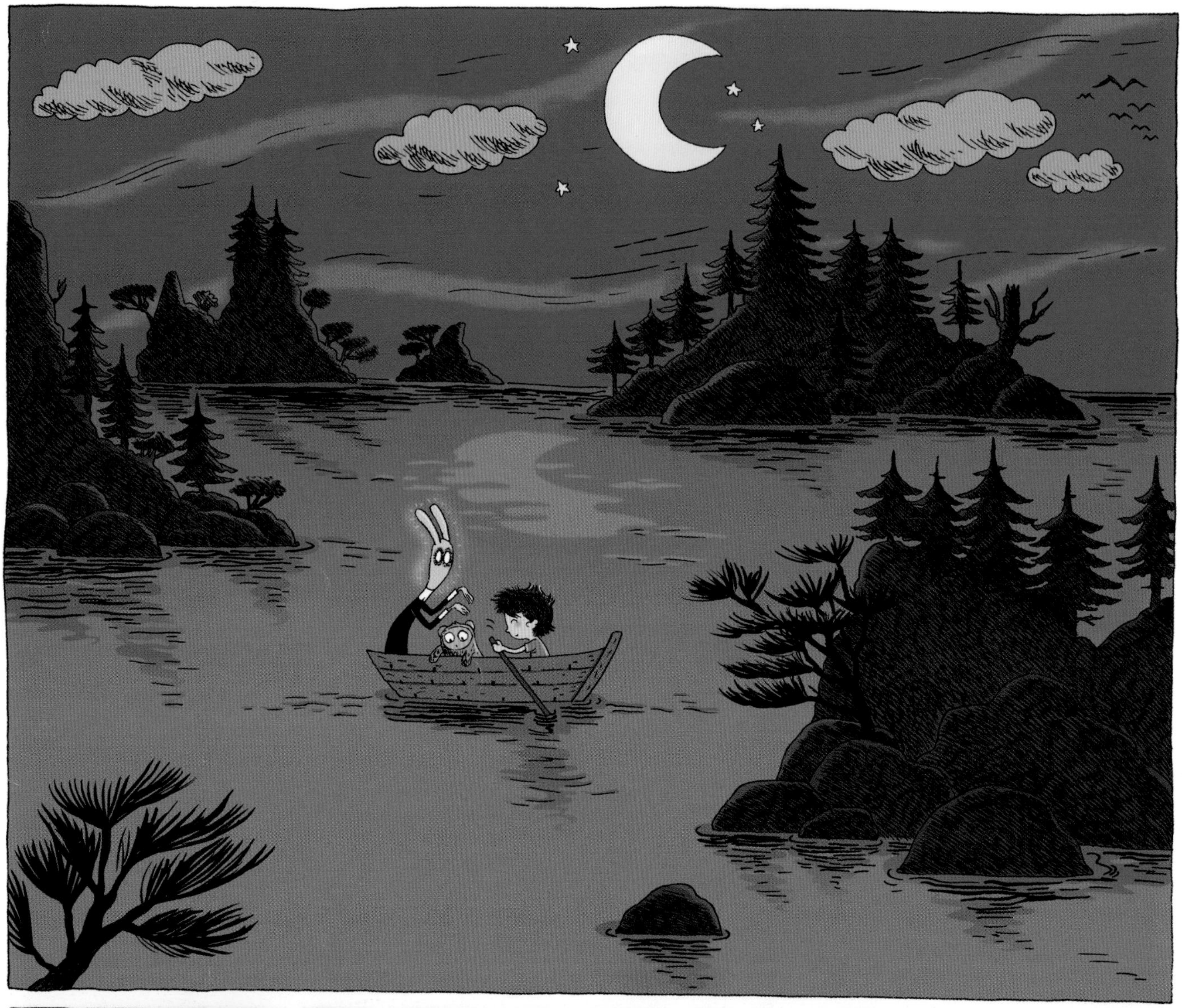

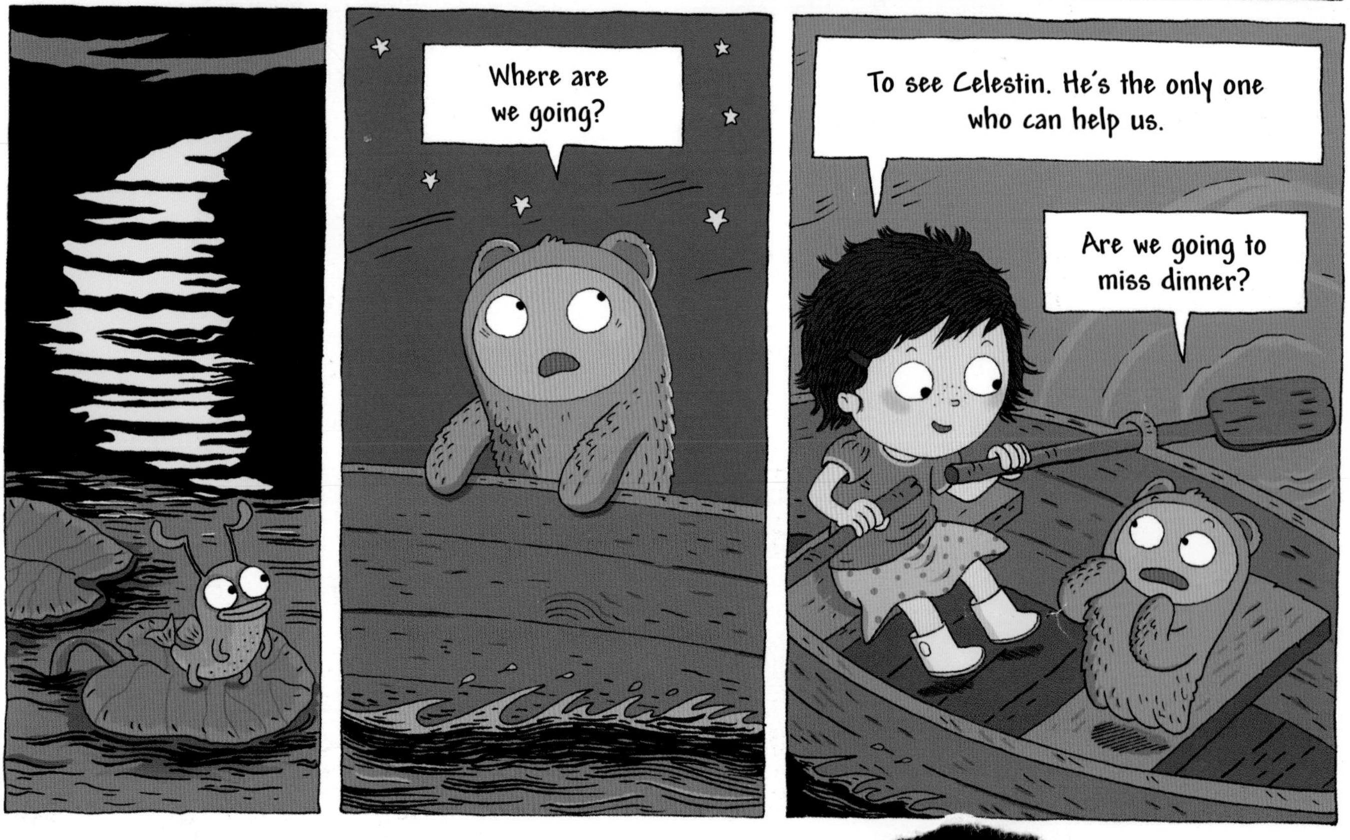
Where are we going?
To see Celestin. He's the only one who can help us.
Are we going to miss dinner?

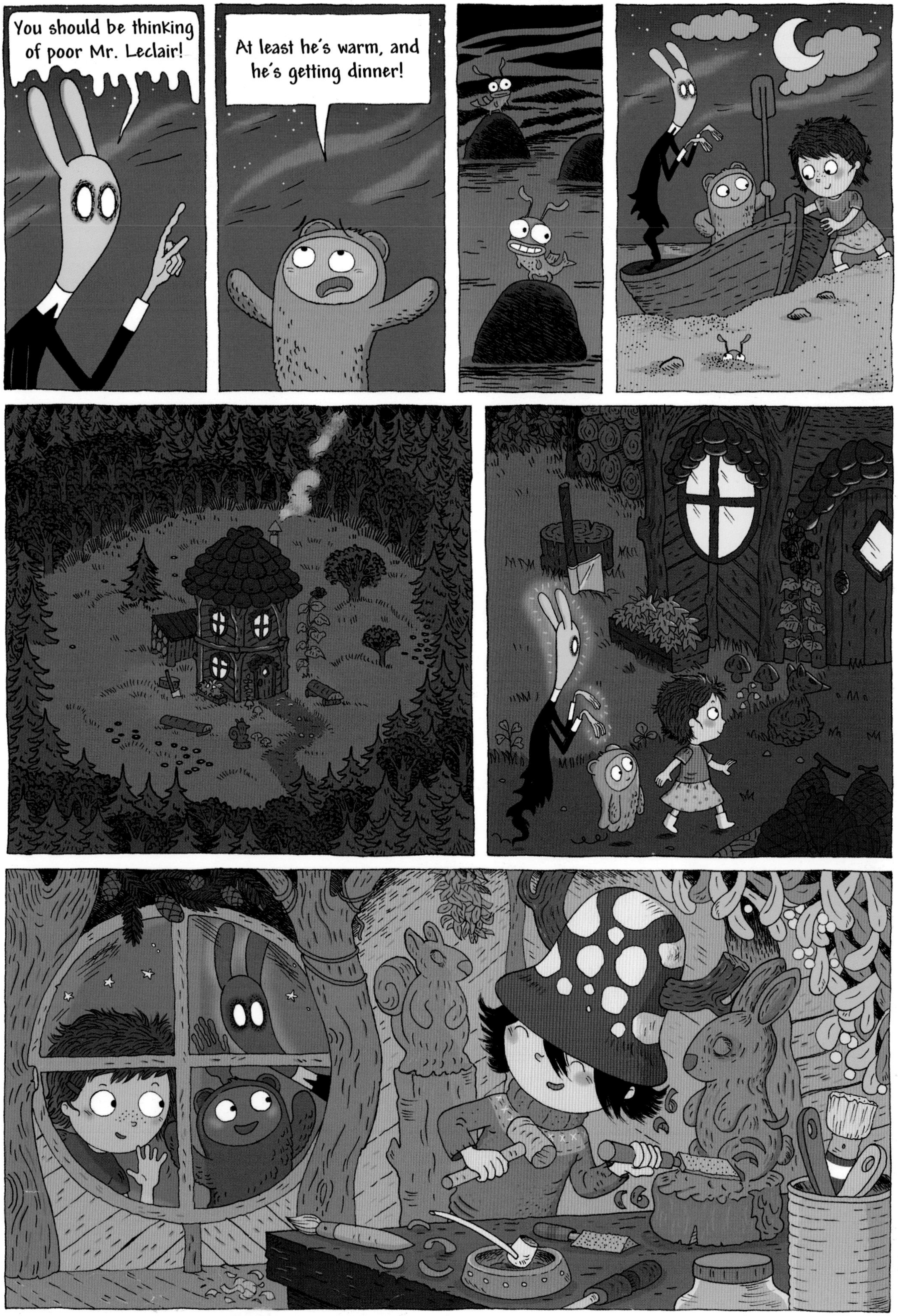
You should be thinking of poor Mr. Leclair!
At least he's warm, and he's getting dinner!

Come in.

I was just making tea.

With cake?

Sure, if you'd like.

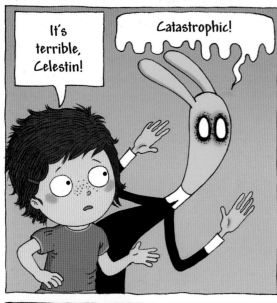

It's terrible, Celestin!

Catastrophic!

We're in trouble with three bandits!

The ones who live in the hollow tree?

Yes, those are the ones!

They never bother me. I don't have anything they'd want.

Someone stole their most beautiful treasure.

It was bound to happen. They have too much wealth for them alone.

22

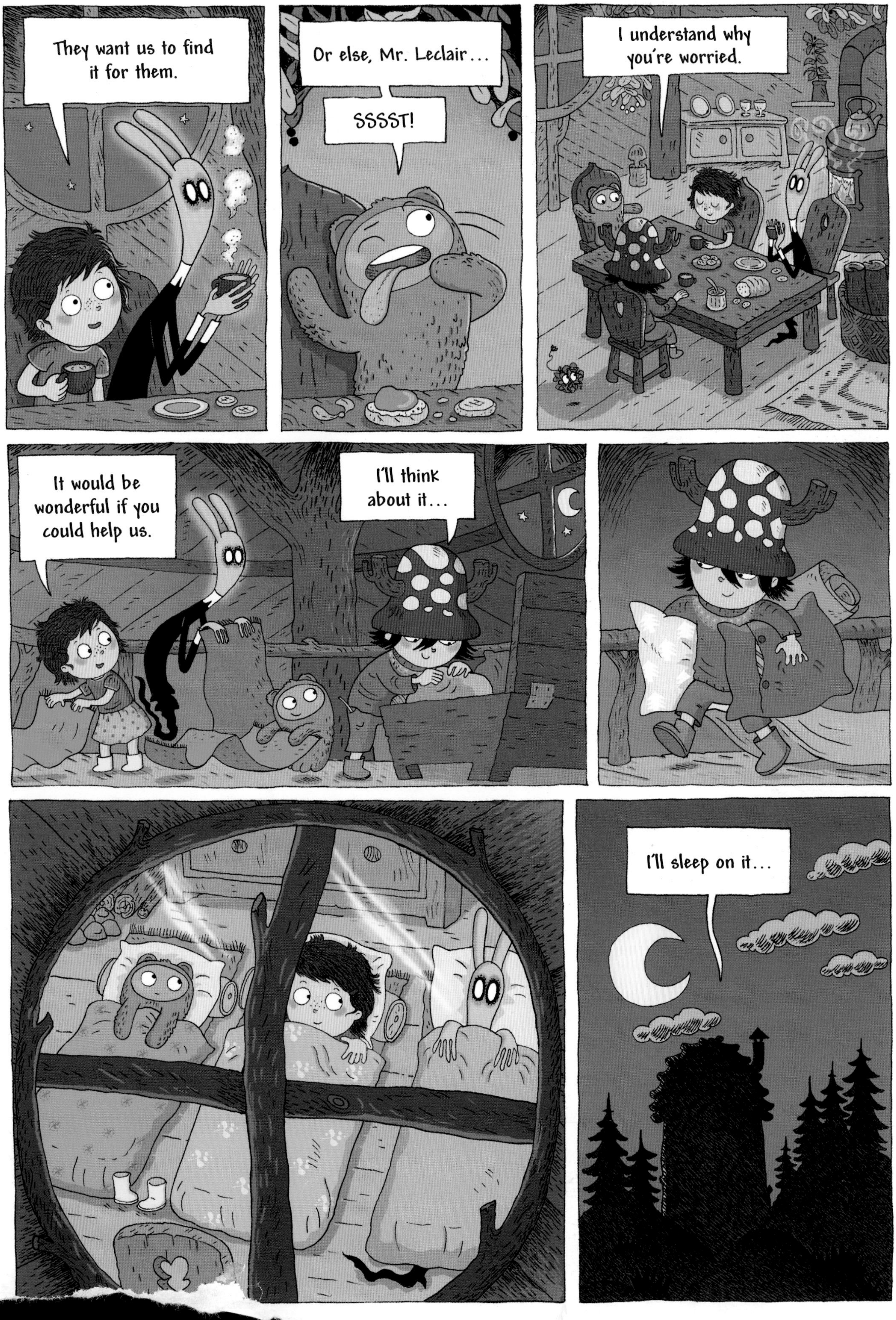
They want us to find it for them.
Or else, Mr. Leclair...
SSSST!
I understand why you're worried.
It would be wonderful if you could help us.
I'll think about it...
I'll sleep on it...

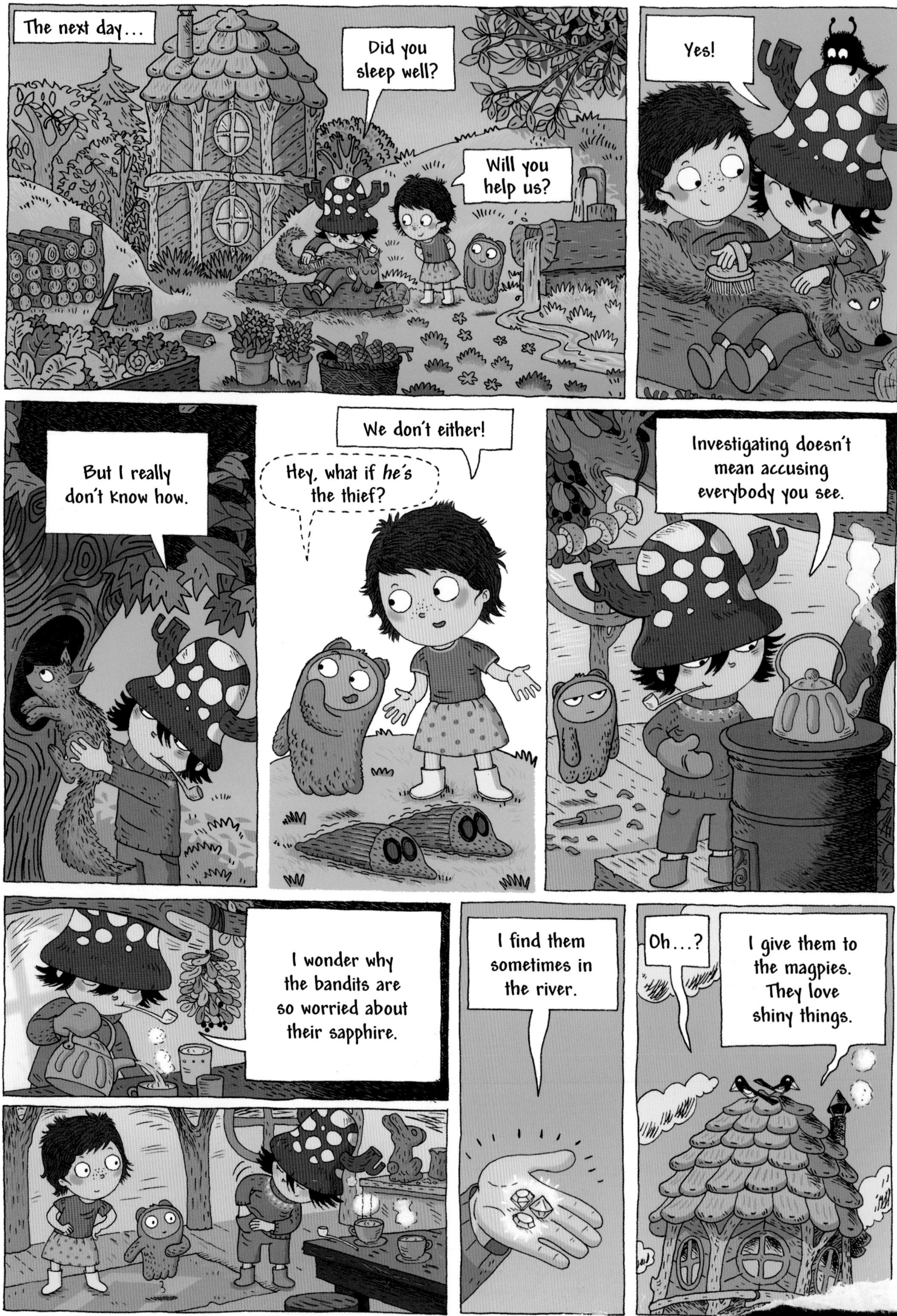
The next day...
Did you sleep well?
Will you help us?
Yes!
But I really don't know how.
Hey, what if *he's* the thief?
We don't either!
Investigating doesn't mean accusing everybody you see.
I wonder why the bandits are so worried about their sapphire.
I find them sometimes in the river.
Oh...?
I give them to the magpies. They love shiny things.

Magpies?

I have an idea!

We let the bandits think we've found their treasure.

And we give them this one. Ta-da! Problem solved.

Heyyy! Thieves!

Let them have fun.

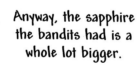

Anyway, the sapphire the bandits had is a whole lot bigger.

If we want to help Mr. Leclair, let's find their sapphire. We'll start the search at your place.

That's silly!

Here comes the husband of the queen.

—of the queen.

—of the queen.

It's the king!

We shouldn't disturb our guests while they're rehearsing.

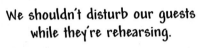

Let's search inside.

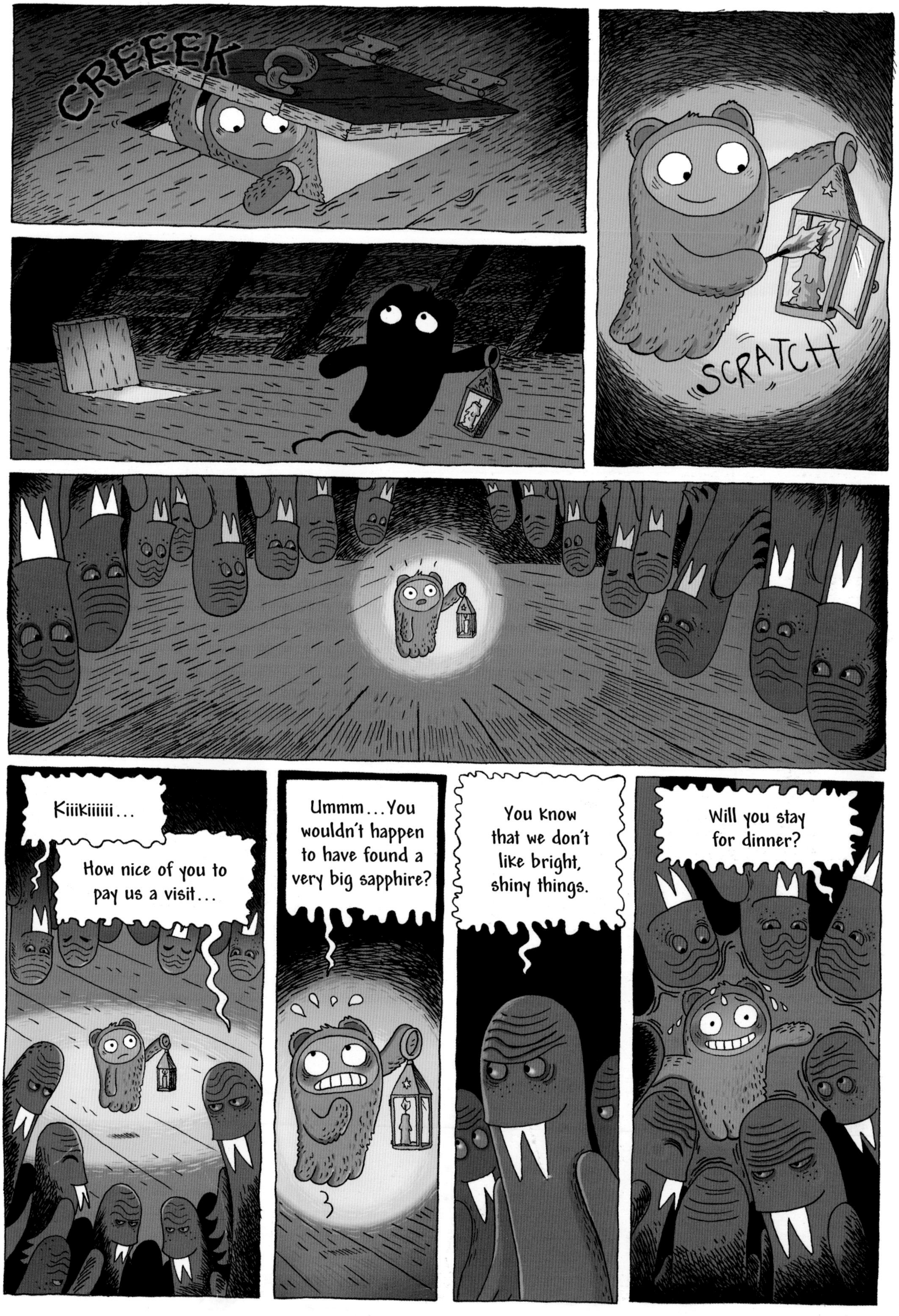
CREEEK
SCRATCH
Kiiikiiiii...
How nice of you to pay us a visit...
Ummm...You wouldn't happen to have found a very big sapphire?
You know that we don't like bright, shiny things.
Will you stay for dinner?

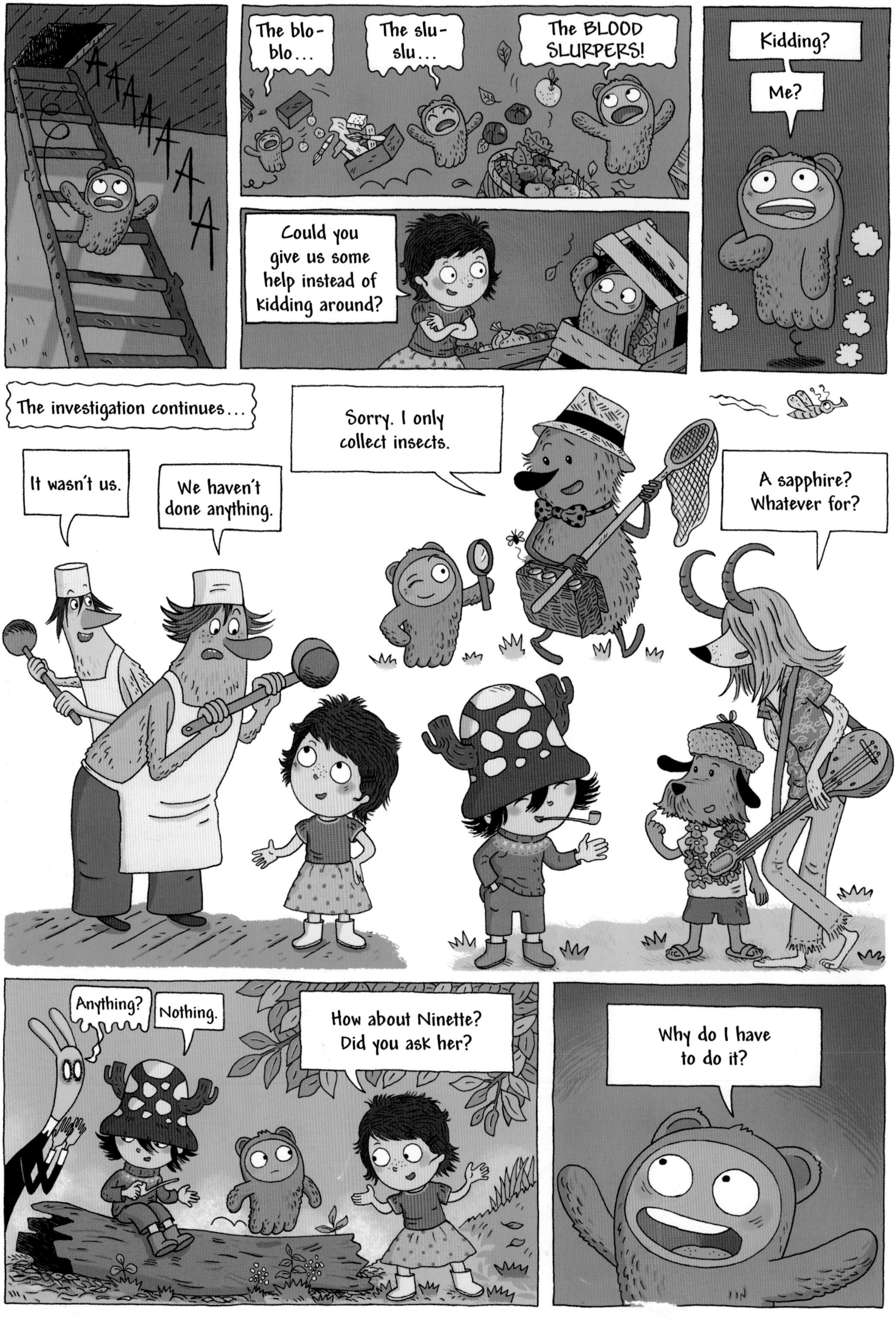
AAAAAAAA
The blo-blo...
The slu-slu...
The BLOOD SLURPERS!
Could you give us some help instead of kidding around?
Kidding?
Me?
The investigation continues...
It wasn't us.
We haven't done anything.
Sorry. I only collect insects.
A sapphire? Whatever for?
Anything?
Nothing.
How about Ninette? Did you ask her?
Why do I have to do it?

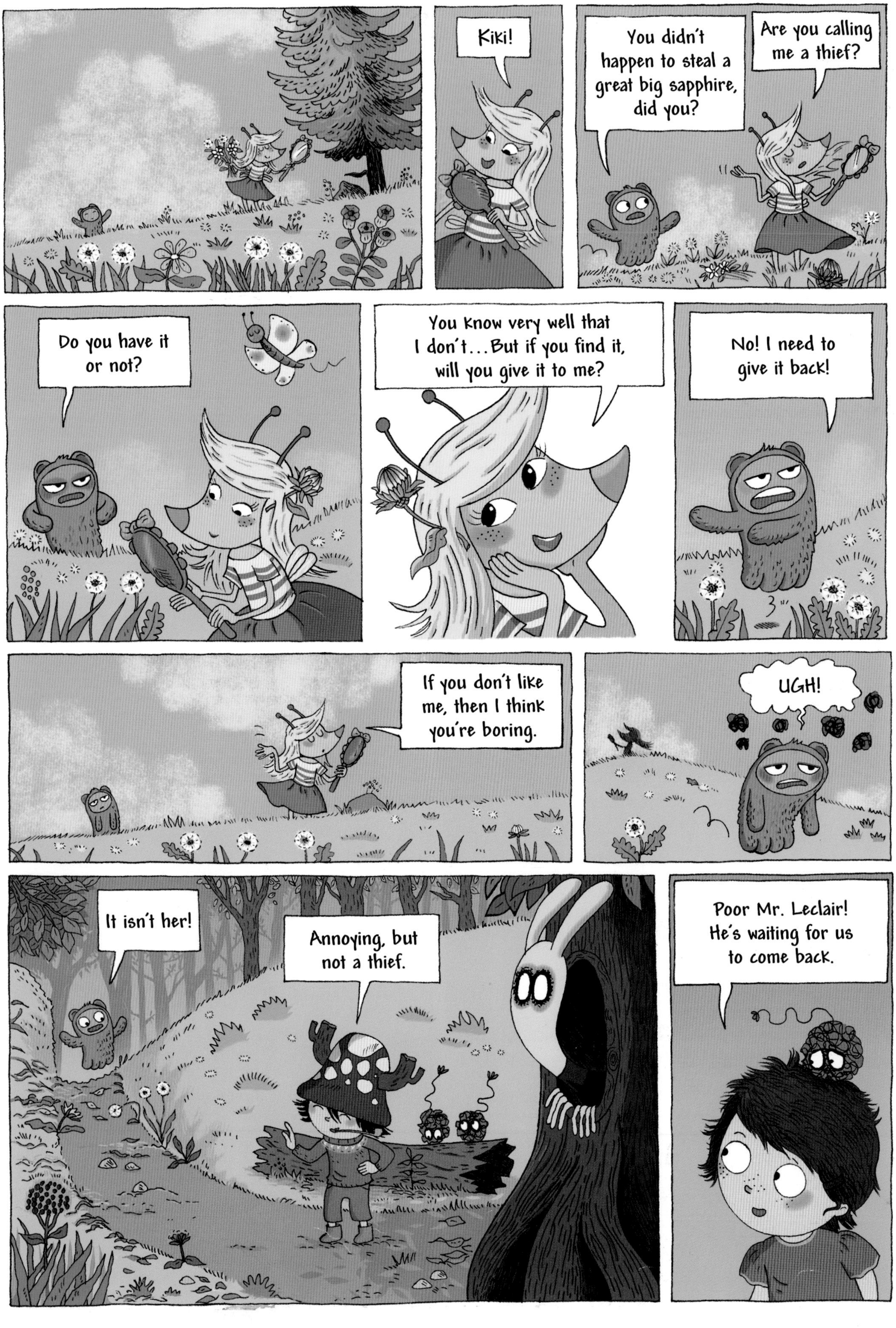

Kiki!
You didn't happen to steal a great big sapphire, did you?
Are you calling me a thief?
Do you have it or not?
You know very well that I don't... But if you find it, will you give it to me?
No! I need to give it back!
If you don't like me, then I think you're boring.
UGH!
It isn't her!
Annoying, but not a thief.
Poor Mr. Leclair! He's waiting for us to come back.

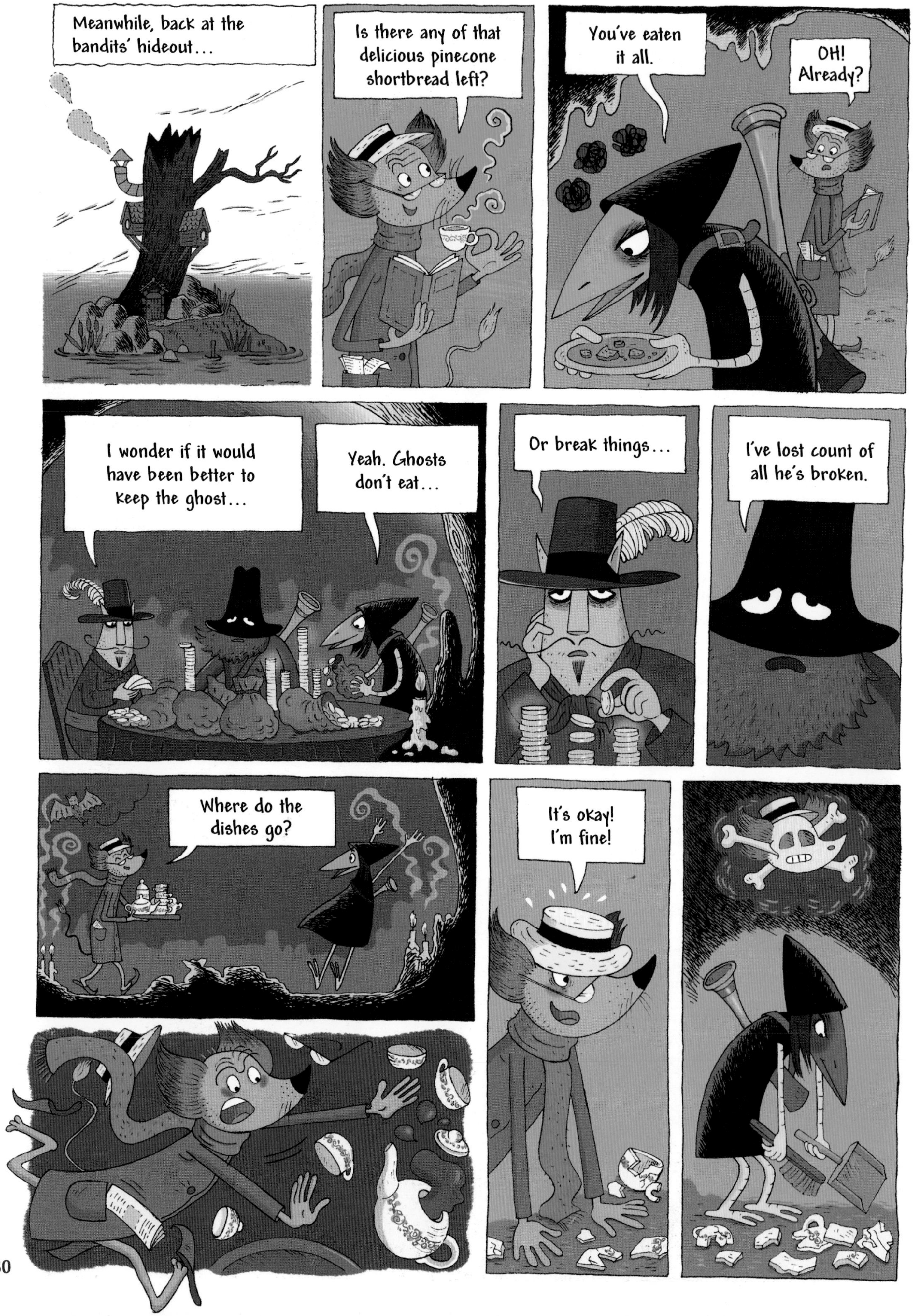
Meanwhile, back at the bandits' hideout...
Is there any of that delicious pinecone shortbread left?
You've eaten it all.
OH! Already?
I wonder if it would have been better to keep the ghost...
Yeah. Ghosts don't eat...
Or break things...
I've lost count of all he's broken.
Where do the dishes go?
It's okay! I'm fine!

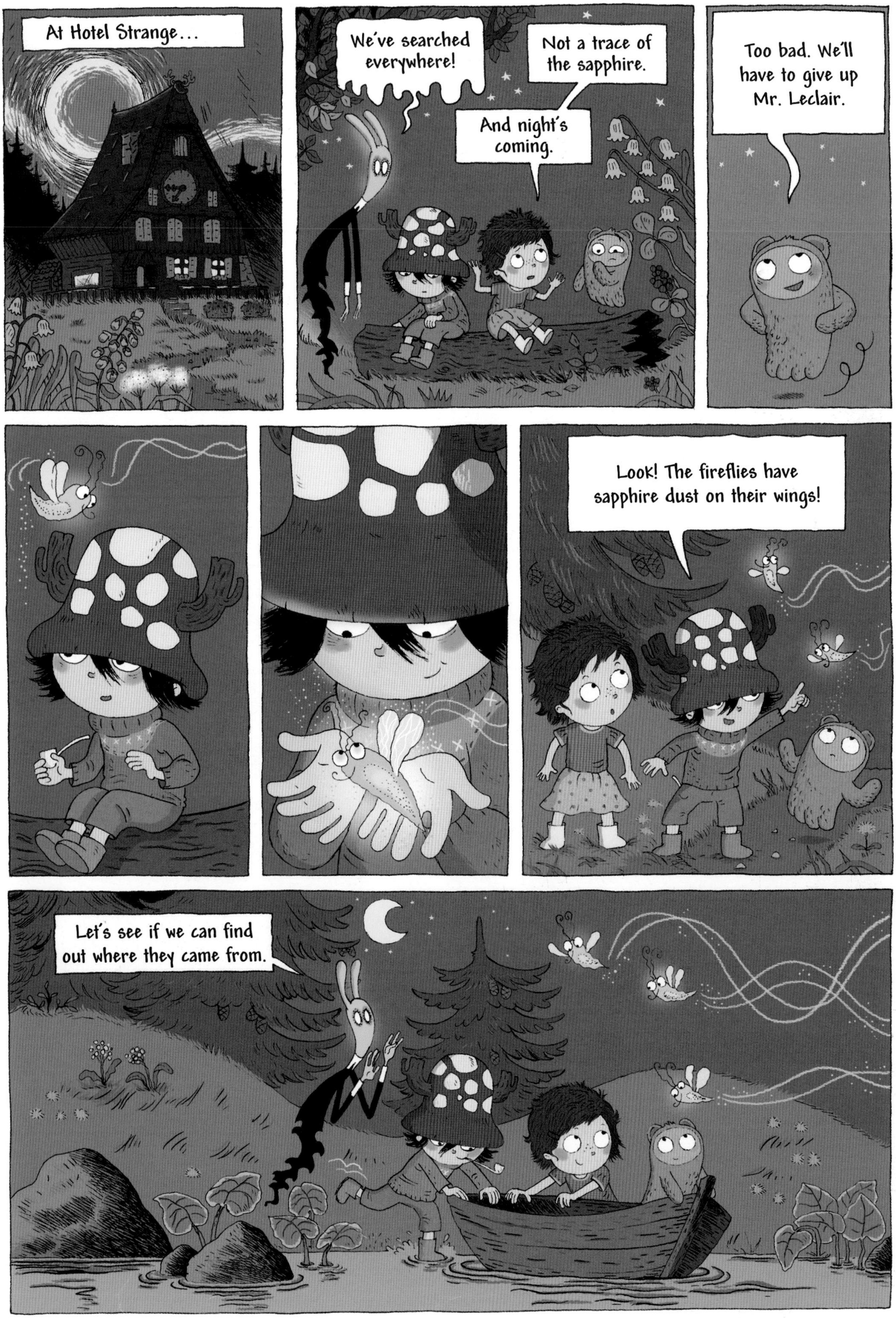
At Hotel Strange...
We've searched everywhere!
Not a trace of the sapphire.
And night's coming.
Too bad. We'll have to give up Mr. Leclair.
Look! The fireflies have sapphire dust on their wings!
Let's see if we can find out where they came from.

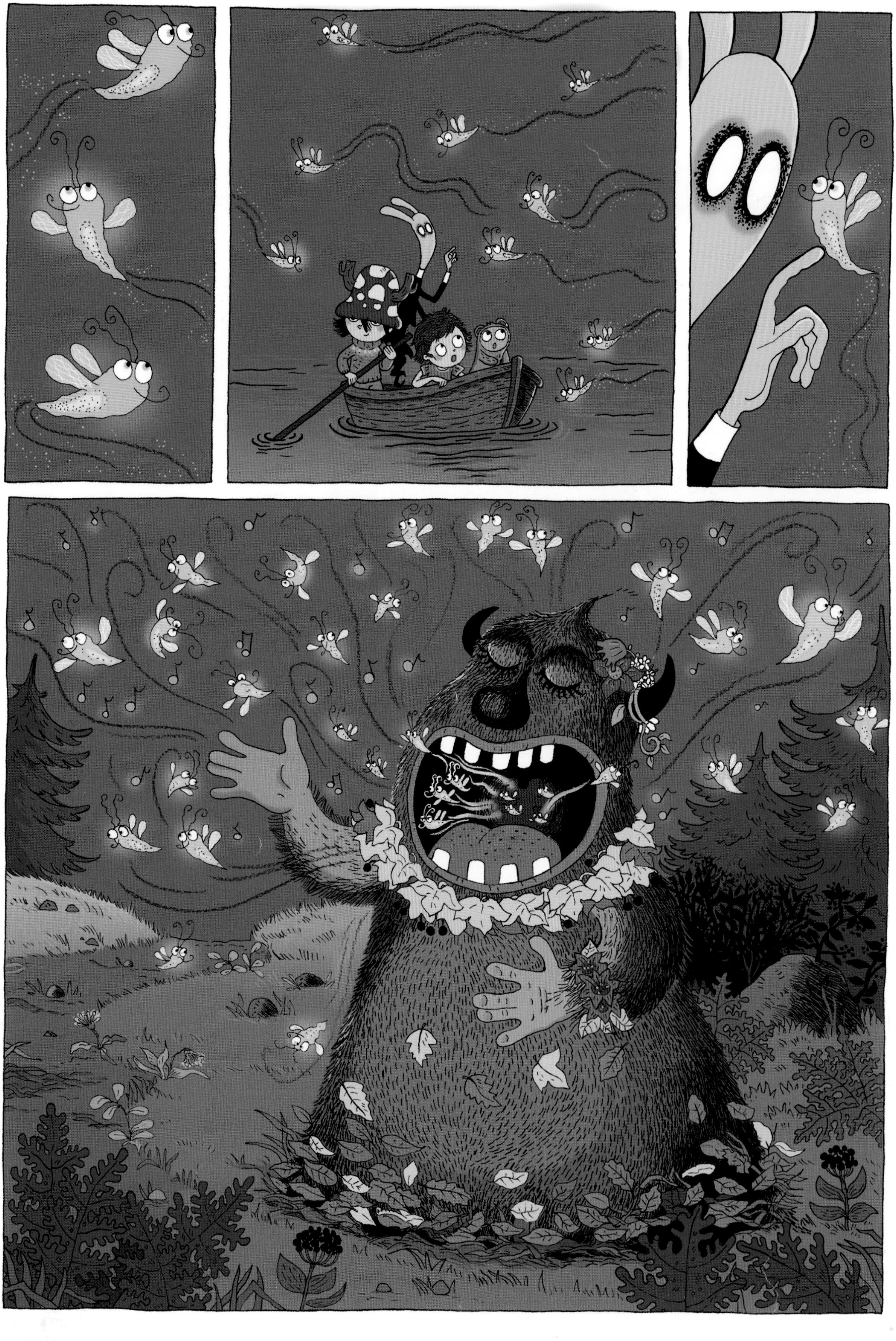

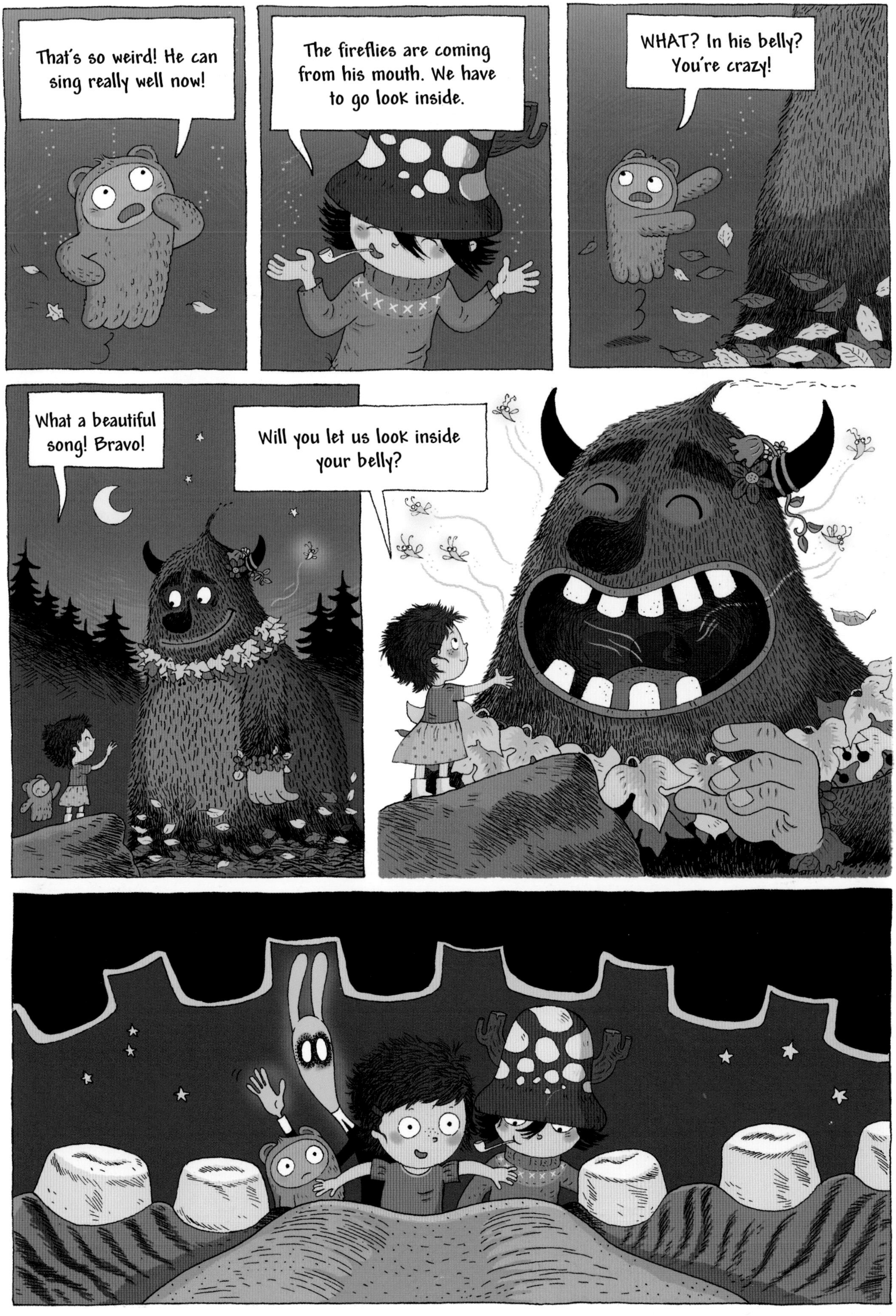
That's so weird! He can sing really well now!
The fireflies are coming from his mouth. We have to go look inside.
WHAT? In his belly? You're crazy!
What a beautiful song! Bravo!
Will you let us look inside your belly?

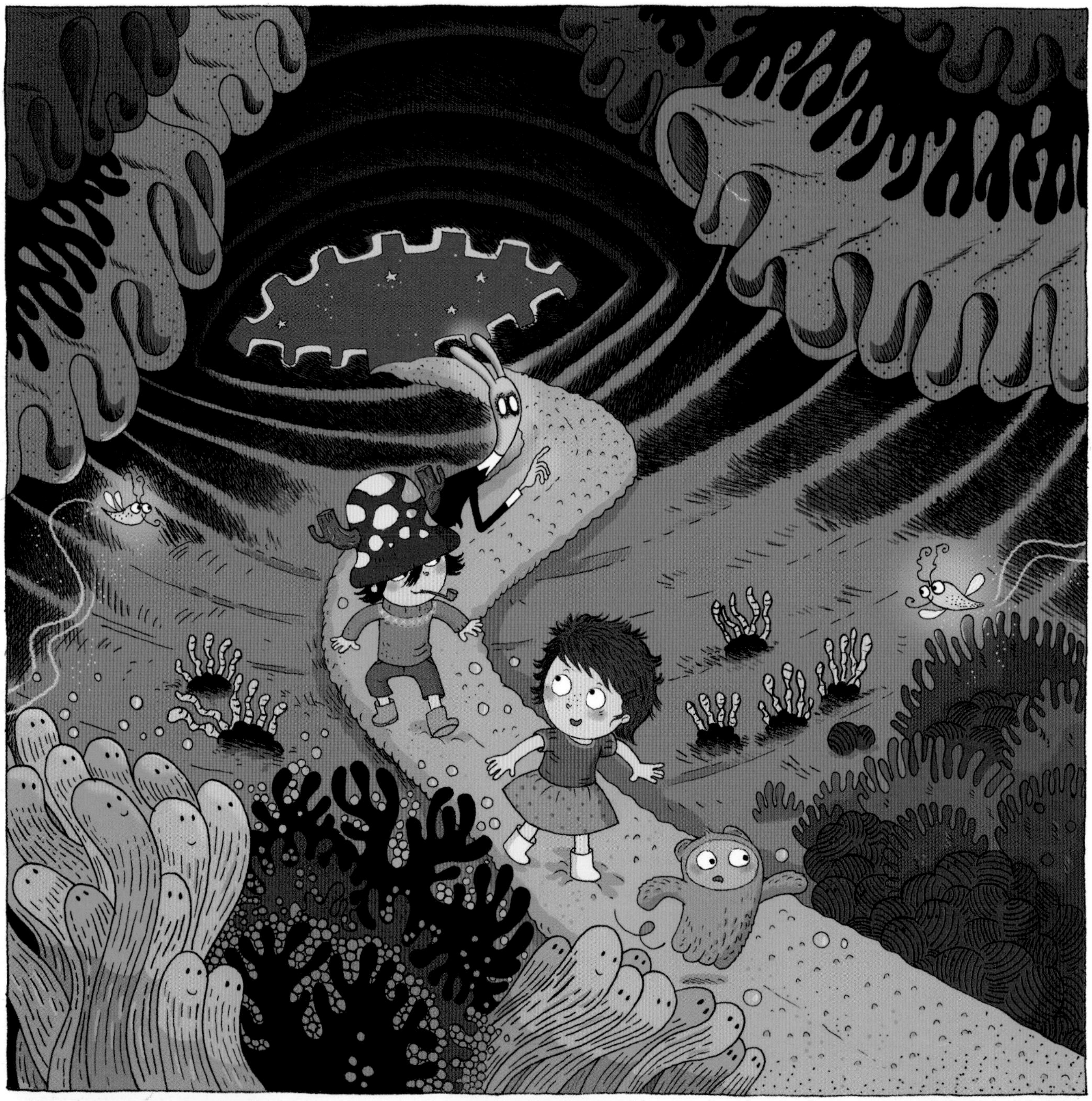

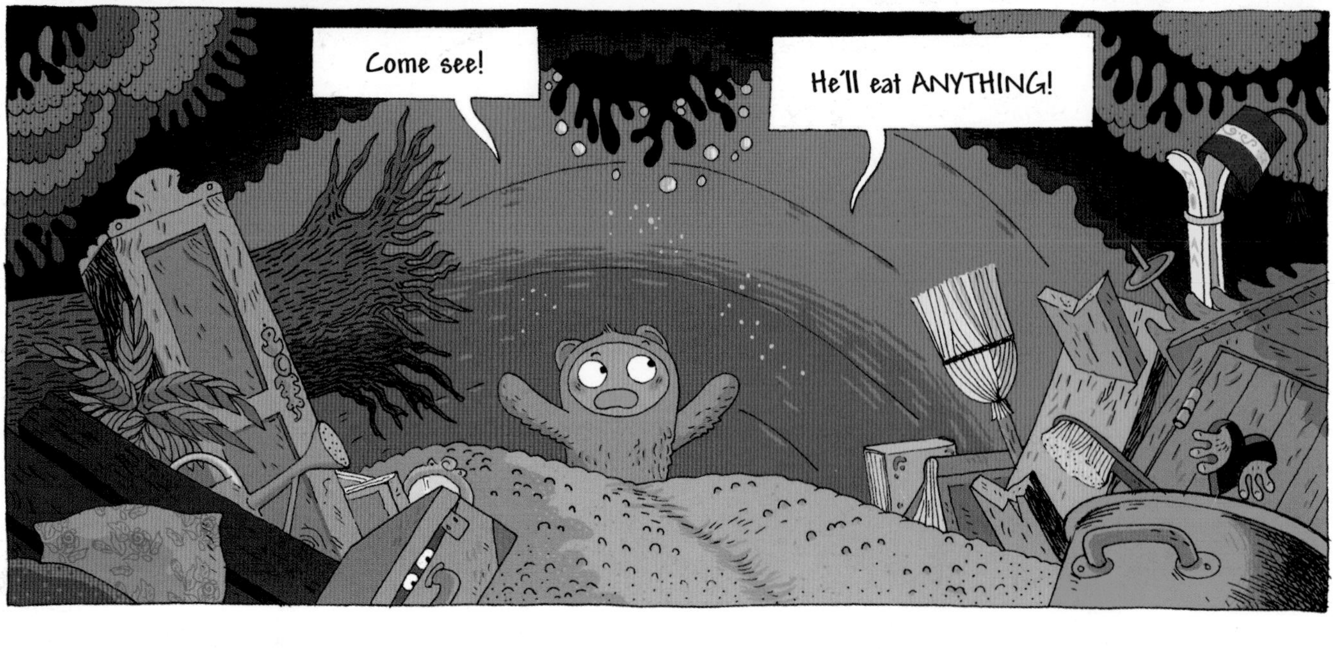
Come see!
He'll eat ANYTHING!

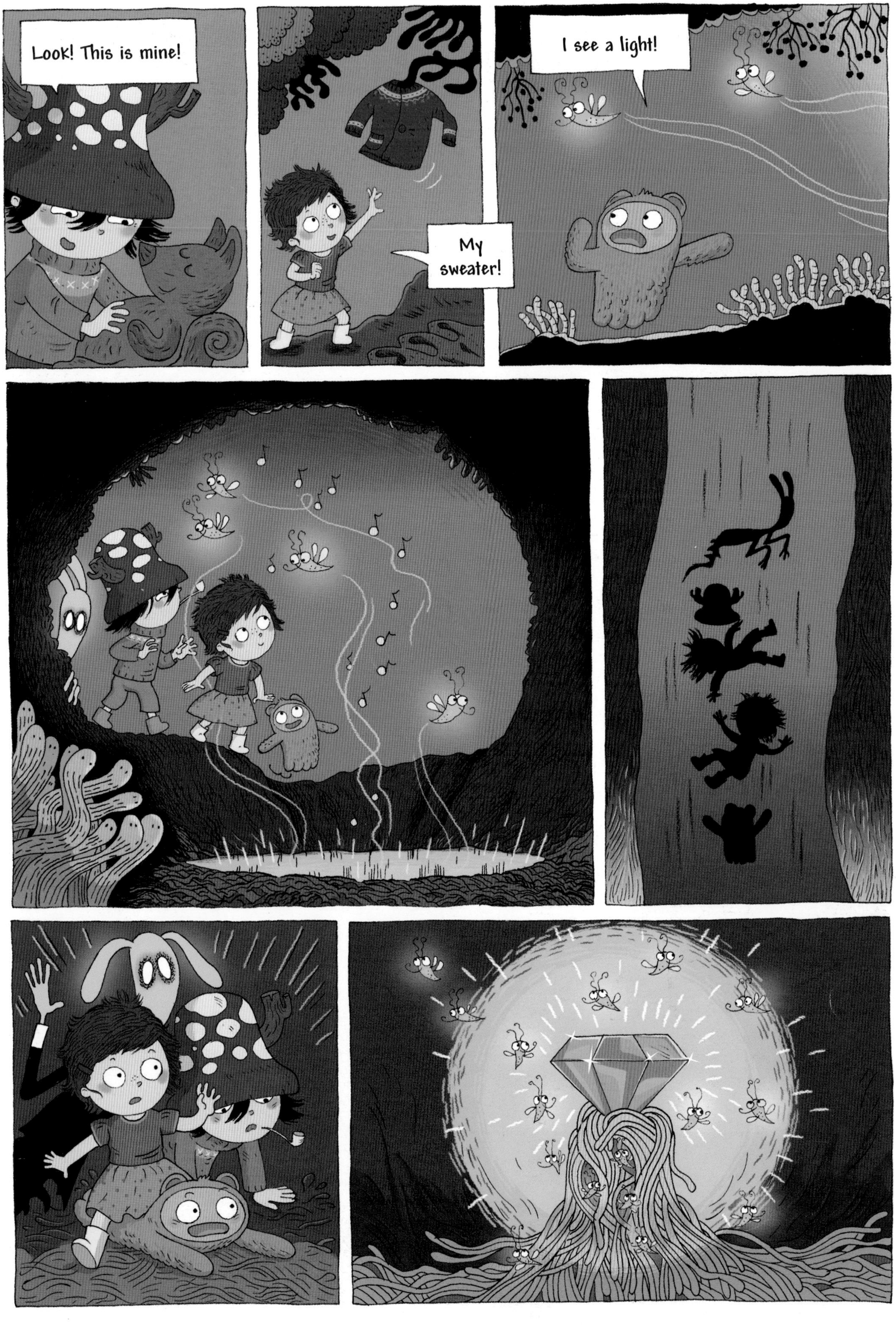
Look! This is mine!
My sweater!
I see a light!

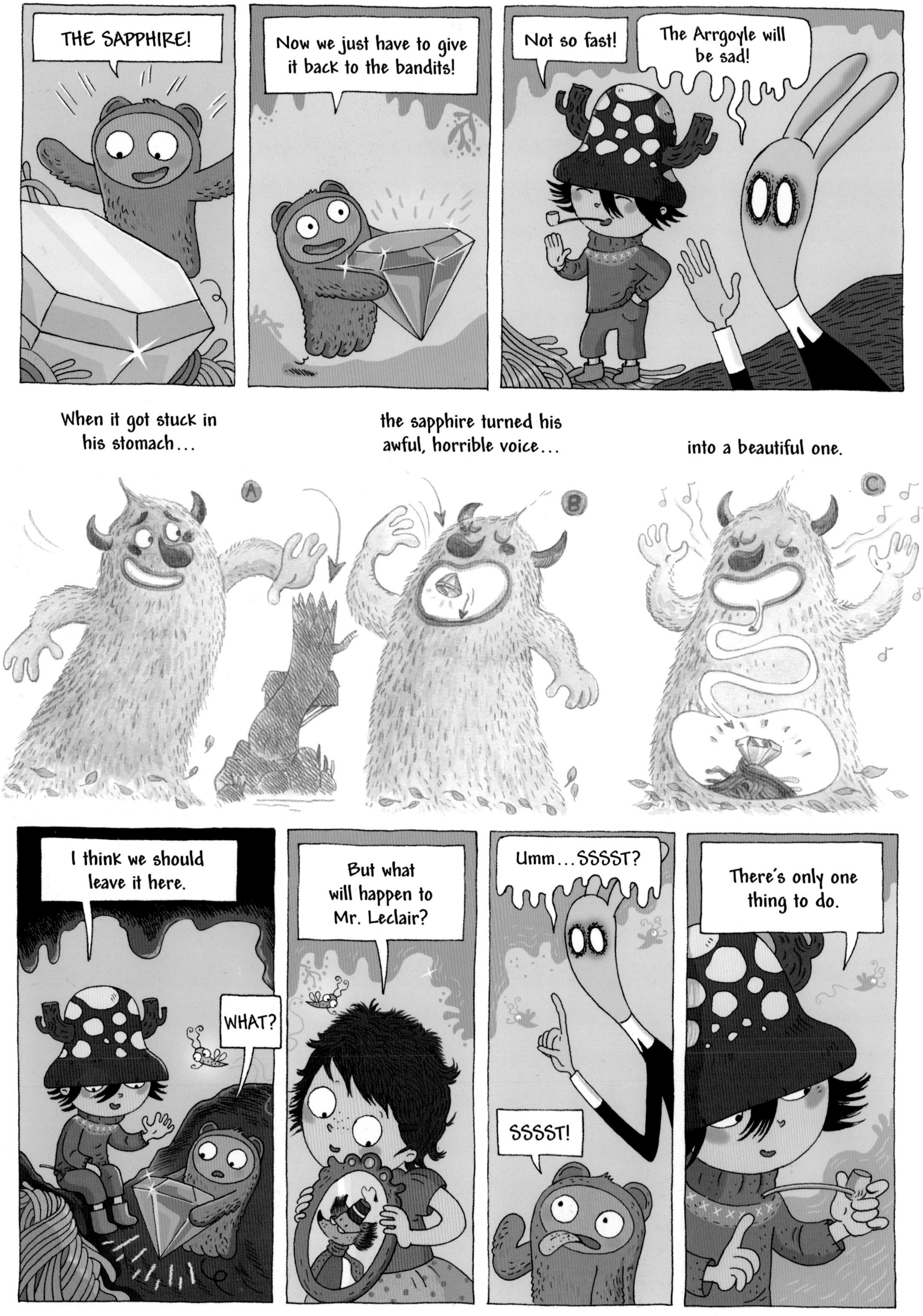
THE SAPPHIRE!
Now we just have to give it back to the bandits!
Not so fast!
The Arrgoyle will be sad!
When it got stuck in his stomach...
the sapphire turned his awful, horrible voice...
into a beautiful one.
A
B
C
I think we should leave it here.
WHAT?
But what will happen to Mr. Leclair?
Umm...SSSST?
SSSST!
There's only one thing to do.

OH! You're finally back!

Mr. Leclair!

HURRAH! The sapphire!

WAAA WAAA WAAA AAAH AAAAH

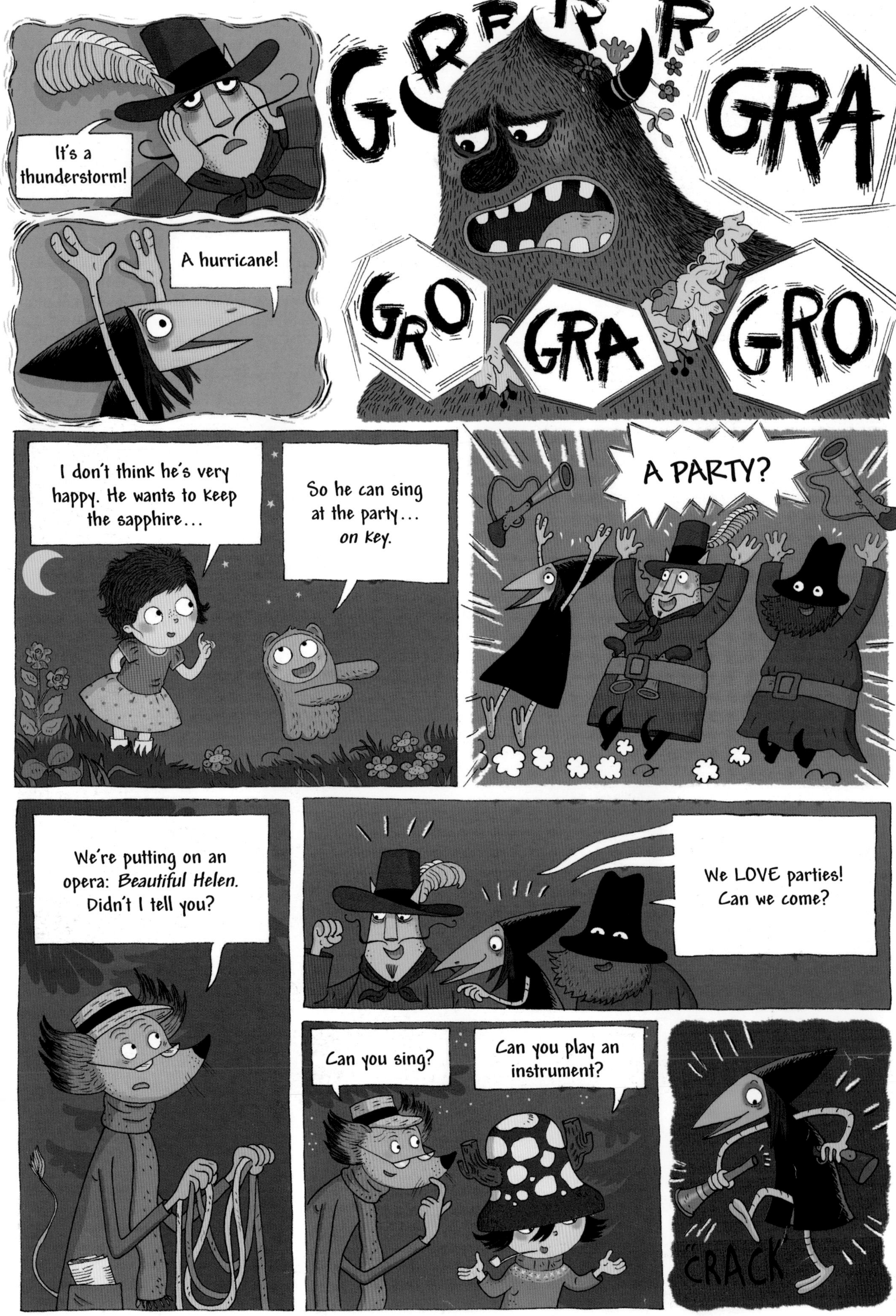

It's a thunderstorm!
A hurricane!
GRRRRR
GRA
GRO
GRA
GRO
I don't think he's very happy. He wants to keep the sapphire...
So he can sing at the party... on key.
A PARTY?
We're putting on an opera: *Beautiful Helen.* Didn't I tell you?
We LOVE parties! Can we come?
Can you sing?
Can you play an instrument?
CRACK

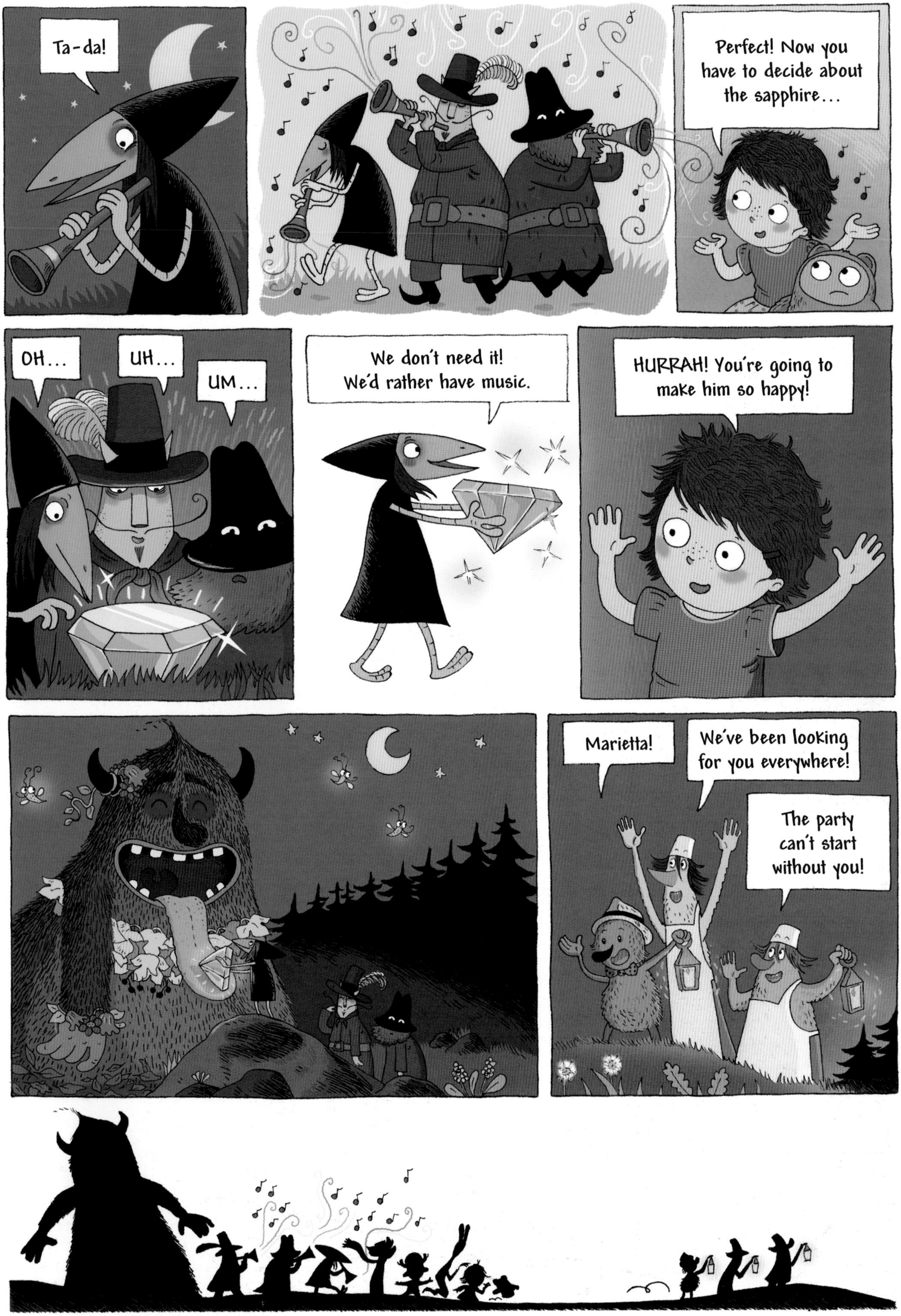
Ta-da!
Perfect! Now you have to decide about the sapphire...
OH...
UH...
UM...
We don't need it! We'd rather have music.
HURRAH! You're going to make him so happy!
Marietta!
We've been looking for you everywhere!
The party can't start without you!

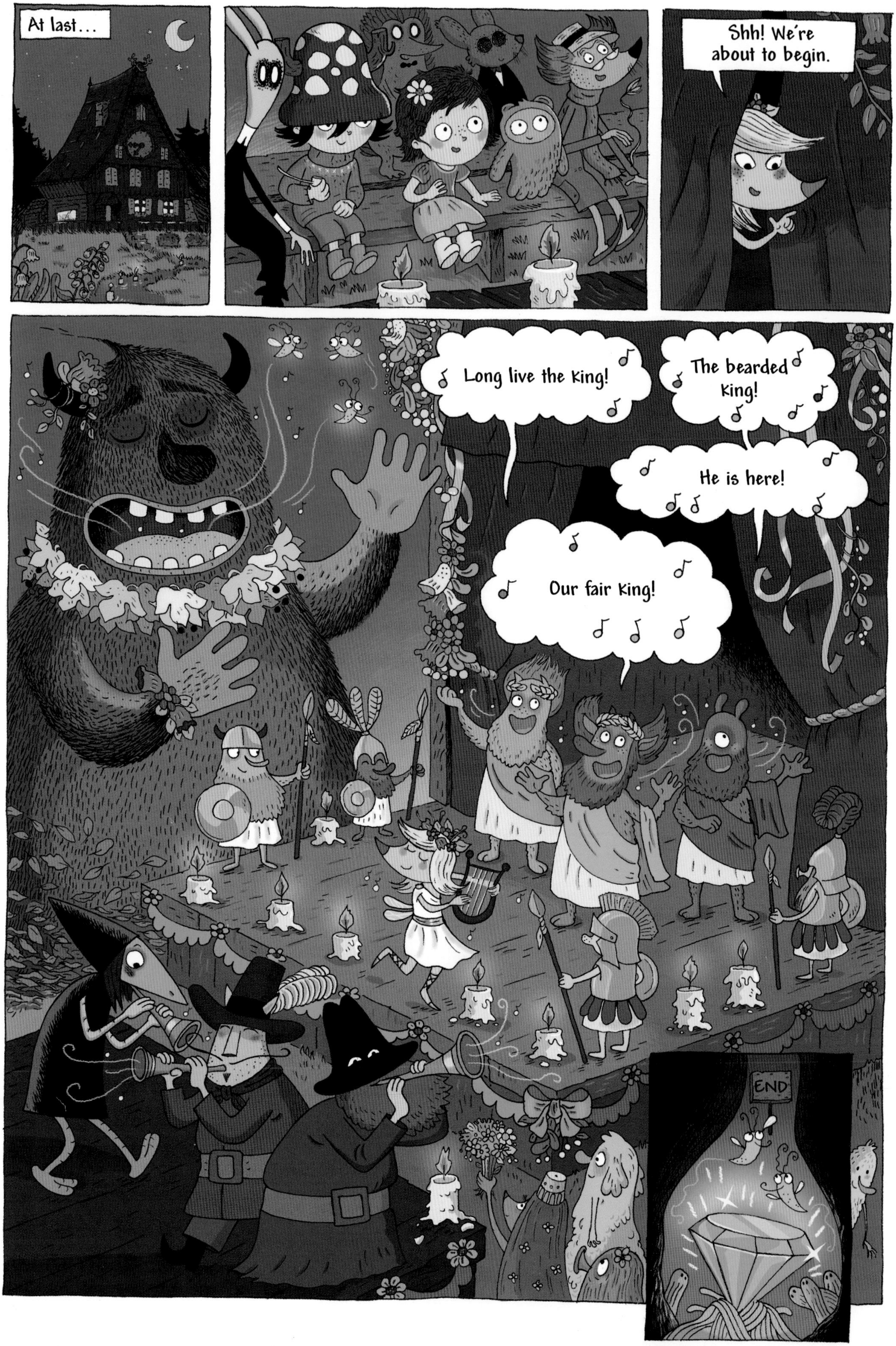
At last...
Shh! We're about to begin.
Long live the king!
The bearded king!
He is here!
Our fair king!
END

Orange Cookies

Ask an adult for help in the kitchen.

Cookies:
3¾ cups all-purpose flour plus
    additional for rolling out dough
½ teaspoon salt
1 cup plus 2 tablespoons sugar
1¼ teaspoons baking powder

2 sticks (8 ounces) softened butter
2 tablespoons orange extract
1 egg
1 tablespoon milk

Glaze:
1 egg yolk plus 1 tablespoon milk

1. Preheat the oven to 400°F.
2. Mix the flour, salt, sugar, and baking powder in a bowl.
3. Add the softened butter. Mix.
4. Add the orange extract. Mix.
5. Add the whole egg and a tablespoon of milk. Mix.
6. Form the dough into a ball.
7. Roll out the dough on a floured surface until it is less than ¼ inch
   (½ centimeter) thick. Cut out circles with a cookie cutter.
8. Arrange the circles on baking sheets lined with parchment paper.
9. Mix the egg yolk and milk to make the glaze. Spread the glaze on the
   cookies using a brush or spoon.
10. Put the cookies in the oven and bake for 10 to 12 minutes.
11. Remove the cookies from the oven, let cool, and store in an airtight
    container.

Makes 24 cookies. They will last at least a week…unless you eat them all first!

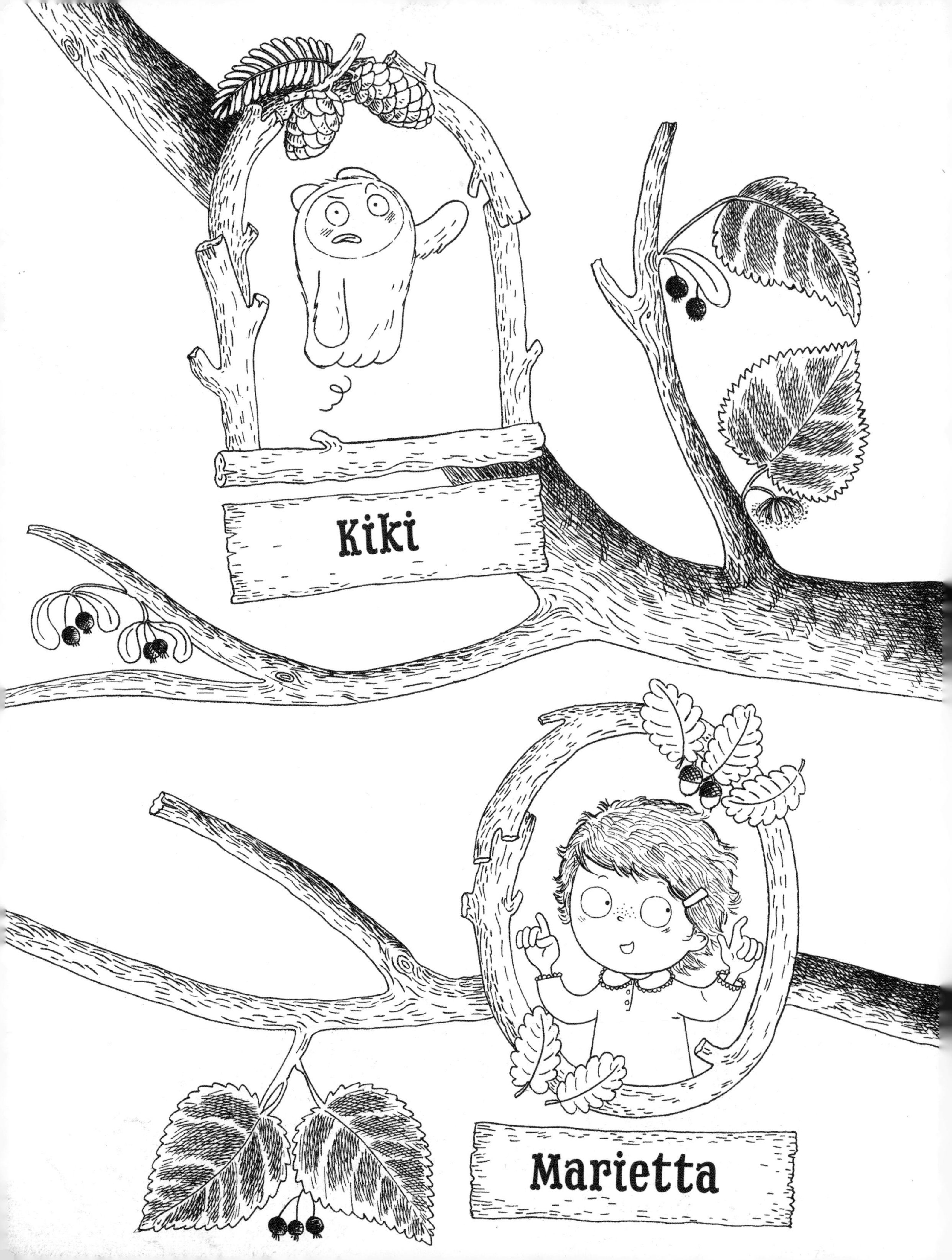
Kiki
Marietta

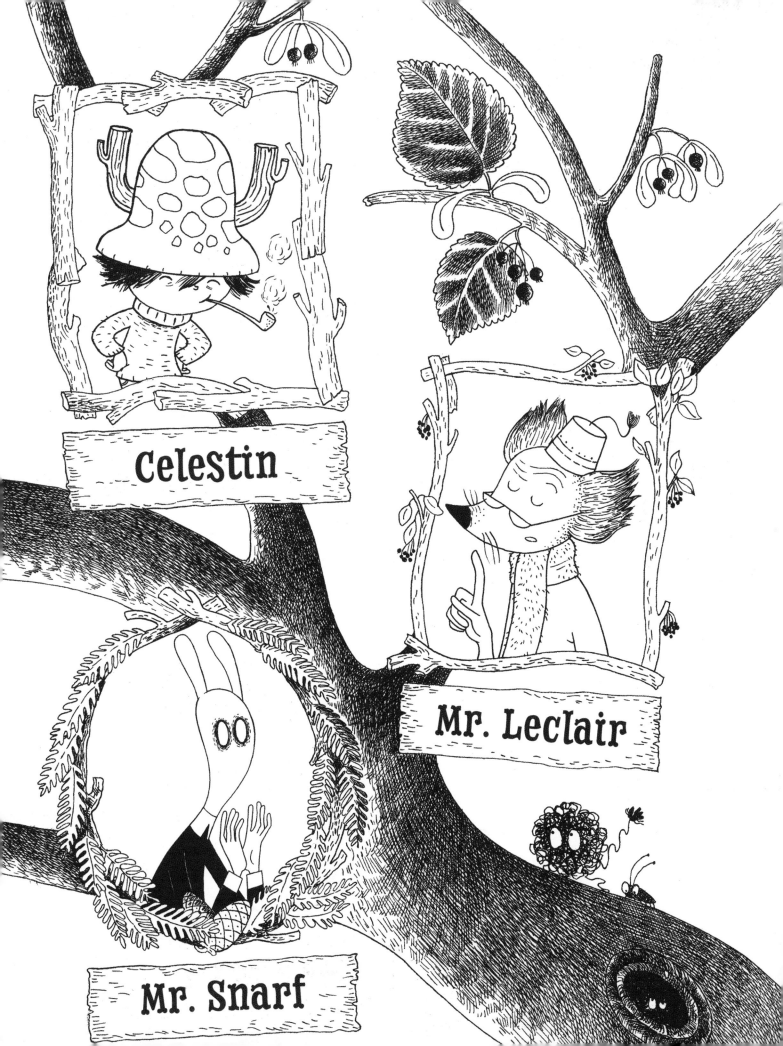

Celestin

Mr. Leclair

Mr. Snarf